Elder Futhark Runes

Unlocking Rune Divination, Norse Magic, Spells, and Runic Symbols

Your Free Gift
(only available for a limited time)

Thanks for getting this book! If you want to learn more about various spirituality topics, then join Mari Silva's community and get a free guided meditation MP3 for awakening your third eye. This guided meditation mp3 is designed to open and strengthen ones third eye so you can experience a higher state of consciousness. Simply visit the link below the image to get started.

https://spiritualityspot.com/meditation

Table of Contents

Introduction

The runes of Elder Futhark are magical symbols that convey the story of life from its first-ever creation in the Universe to the birth, death, and rebirth of every living being. According to Norse mythology, these forces constantly occur in nature and are also present in all aspects of magic. The Germanic tribes living in Northern Europe centuries ago discovered that runes provided an outlet for natural magic. They also used them as tools to harness natural energy.

This book will help you understand that the Norse runes' magic is not limited by the symbolism of any individual rune. In addition, the meanings of each of the runes are also tied to the meaning of other runes. Elder Futhark runes were initially nothing but a series of sounds, often described as incantations. They were also used to communicate with the spiritual world and nature and express gratitude. All these aspects are valuable tools for a contemporary Norse magic practitioner, regardless of their experience level.

This book will teach you how to use Norse runes in reverse order compared to how they were discovered. Instead of writing down the symbols after familiarizing yourself with their concept as it happened through the centuries, you will first practice writing them as a way to familiarize yourself with their meaning. This is where the user-friendly practical portion of the book will come in handy. This will teach you how to equate the 24 runes of the Elder Futhark with the letters of the Latin alphabet, beginning with F and ending with O.

After practicing their written form, you'll be ready to move on to learn about the three purposes of the runes - communication, divination, and invocations. The second half of this book provides plenty of hands-on techniques to incorporate these intentions into your practice. Not only that, but it'll also enlist all the different meanings associated with each rune.

The number of ways you incorporate Norse runes into magical practices is infinite. This has become more than evident through the recent revival of Asatru, Odinism, and similar Norse magic approaches. Whatever your Norse magic practice entails, expanding your knowledge about the Elder Futhark runes will allow you to access new avenues for divination, spells, and more.

Being the oldest form of the runic alphabet, Elder Futhark represents the gateway to the most elemental and empowering form of magic. So, if you are ready to empower yourself through Norse runes, keep reading. You'll uncover a world that makes using natural magic as easy as breathing. Once you familiarize yourself with all the runic symbolism and learn to create your own, finding ways to enrich your practice will be one of your biggest strengths. After all, divination, spells, spiritual communication, and rituals aren't the only ways to harness energy through runes. You can also incorporate them into your meditation exercises, use them as protection while you sleep, or even wear them as jewelry and other forms of talismans. With all these ways to make you more aware of Norse magic, it's up to you how and when you start implementing them!

Chapter 1: Introduction to Norse Mythology

We can't talk about Elder Futhark runes without mentioning their origin, which was Norse mythology. You may be familiar with Norse mythology since the Marvel characters Thor, Loki, and Odin were all inspired by it. English author Neil Gaiman was also inspired by Norse mythology and wrote a book under the same name. Many of the characters from his novel "American gods" (later turned into a TV show) were based on Norse gods like Loki and Odin. Another English author heavily influenced by Norse mythology is J. R. R. Tolkien, especially in his popular novels Lord of the Rings and The Hobbit. Norse mythology found its way to modern culture along with the Vikings, or Norsemen, portrayed in various movies and TV shows.

The Vikings were a group of people from various countries like Iceland, Norway, Sweden, and Denmark who followed the Norse pagan religion. They were explorers, traders, conquerors, raiders, and settlers. They lived during the appropriately named "Viking Age" from 793 CE to 1066 CE. They traveled to multiple places outside Europe, like ancient Baghdad and North America, which they discovered centuries before Christopher Columbus was even born. They spoke the Old Norse language, a Germanic language, and wrote in runes which we will discuss in detail in the coming chapters.

Various reasons led the Vikings to move from their homeland and conquer the world. However, what they desired more than anything was wealth and power. They left us with many poems, legends, and sagas of their lives during Pre-Christian times. In fact, we know more about the Vikings' religion than any other Germanic religion. However, all Germanic religions shared some similarities with Norse Paganism.

Although Greek and Roman mythologies and their gods are more popular, this doesn't make Norse mythology and its gods and legends any less fascinating. As more and more people discover Norse mythology, its popularity grows, which has left its mark on modern civilization. However, if you think you know everything about Norse mythology after watching a movie or a TV show, we are here to tell you that the real legends are much more fascinating. This chapter will focus on Norse mythology and uncover its many secrets.

What Is Norse Mythology?

We may think we know that Norse mythology was based on what we know about its fearless warriors, the Vikings, or its popular gods, Thor and Loki. However, there is more to it than what is portrayed in modern culture. A big part of Norse mythology was its religion and the various beliefs heavily practiced and followed by European Germanics. The tribes residing in northern and central Europe at the time all practiced the same Norse religion and spoke the same Norse languages. Although various cultures practiced Christianity during the middle ages, the Norsemen remained true to their pagan religion and beliefs.

The Norse religion wasn't different from other religions as it was also based on stories that taught the people moral lessons and helped them understand and learn about the world around them. Norse mythology is a collection of stories and tales of various gods and goddesses. The Vikings found meaning in these stories as they provided them with the wisdom and guidance they needed to live their lives. The Vikings never gave a proper name to their religions like Christianity, Islam, Buddhism, and various other religions. They simply referred to it as "tradition."

If there is one thing all religions share in common, it's the belief in the divine or greater power, and the Norse religion was no different. It had its own methods of worshiping and connecting to the divine. These methods may seem strange and unusual to you at first. However, at their core, they were simply human quests to help people find the joy of being connected to a higher power and live their lives in the presence of the divine. The Vikings saw their world differently. They found everything, whether their culture or nature, to be enchanting and marvelous.

For this reason, they never tried to change things and left them the way they were. This isn't to say that Norse mythology painted the world as a perfect place. On the contrary, their myths acknowledge that life could be unfair and full of misfortunes and sadness. How you deal with these challenges and accomplish good deeds for the greater good can help you live a good life and reach Valhalla.

Valhalla is an old Nordic word that means “the hall of the fallen.” It is similar to our modern-day concept of heaven. It is the place or “hall” in the afterlife where Odin (god of the dead and ruler of Valhalla) houses the souls of the dead. It is believed that only brave Viking soldiers who died in battle can go there.

The Vikings didn't just believe in one god. Like the ancient Greeks, Romans, and Egyptians, they believed in various gods and assigned a deity for everything. For instance, Odin was the god of death, Thor was the god of thunder, and Loki was the god of mischief. There were about 66 gods and goddesses the Germanic people believed in. Like in most similar religions, there was also a god who served as the head of all other deities, and Odin filled this role. He was married to the goddess of fertility, Frigg, who became the chief goddess after marrying Odin. They had twin sons, Hodr and Baldur. Odin is believed to have married other goddesses and had many affairs with various other goddesses and giantesses as well, resulting in many children like Thor (the god of thunder), Heimdall (the watcher of Asgard, where the Norse gods reside), Vidar (god of revenge), Bragi (g0d of poetry), Hermodr (messenger 0f the gods), Tyr (the bravest of all gods), and many others. However, unlike in the Marvel movies, Loki wasn't Odin's son; he was a companion to some gods, including Odin and Thor.

The gods weren't represented as perfect beings, but they possessed various human qualities, and some of them were not exactly good, like Loki. To better understand Norse mythology and its various deities, let's look at some of its popular myths.

The Myth of the Death of Baldur

Baldur was the son of Odin and his wife, Frigg. He was very popular, loved, and respected among all the gods. His popularity resulted from his generosity, courage, and joyful personality. Everyone loved spending time with him. Baldur began having nightmares of something terrible befalling him. Many ancient cultures believed that their dreams held meaning back then. As a result, Baldur grew wary and turned to other gods, including his father Odin, to find the meaning behind these dreams.

Odin, concerned about his son, disguised himself and traveled to the underworld to seek the help of a dead seeress. A seeress is a woman who can perform sorcery and foretell the future. The seeress that Odin sought was known for her wisdom and dream interpretation. Upon his arrival at the underworld, Odin noticed that there were decorations and preparations held for a feast. Odin was bewildered and went to the seeress to inquire about the reason behind the festivity. The seeress had no idea that she was talking to the chief god and told him the festivity was held in Baldur's honor. However, this event would not end happily. She informed him that Baldur would meet his demise this evening during these festivities. Suddenly, the seeress fell silent and stopped herself from giving any more information because she realized the man she spoke to was none other than Odin.

Odin was heartbroken over the fate that would befall his son, and he went back to Asgard and shared this information with the other gods. When Frigg learned about the fate that awaited her son, she decided to do everything she could to save him. She went to every living and non-living entity in the universe and made them take an oath to never harm her son. Nothing and no one could touch Baldur now. Even when other gods, in jest, threw rocks at Baldur, he remained unharmed. Neither the rocks nor anyone or anything was breaking their oath.

Loki, who thrived on chaos and mischief, went to Frigg disguised as a woman to find out if all entities had taken the oath not to harm Baldur. Frigg told him that only the mistletoe hadn't taken an oath because it was so small and harmless, and she didn't believe it could hurt her son. Loki found a great opportunity to get rid of Baldur, who he was jealous of. This could have been the result of Baldur's popularity or because Loki enjoyed messing with the gods and watching everyone suffer.

The god of mischief carved a spear out of mistletoe and went to the place where the gods played around with Baldur. They threw things at him so they could see what could hurt him. Hodr, Baldur's twin brother, was blind and couldn't participate in these games. Loki convinced him that he should join the fun. It was also an honor to prove to Baldur how invincible he was. Loki offered to help Hodr to throw the spear in the right direction. Not knowing he was being tricked, Hodr threw the mistletoe spear at his brother, who met his demise on the spot.

This was a terrible incident that left all the gods speechless. They considered the death of Baldur as a sign that would bring about Ragnarok, or the end of the universe. Nana, Baldur's wife, couldn't handle the grief and died during her husband's funeral and was laid to rest by his side. Frigg was understandably heartbroken, but she composed herself to try to find a loyal and brave god who could travel to the underworld and meet the goddess of death, Hel, Loki's daughter. Frigg wanted to offer Hel a reward to bring Baldur and his wife back. Hermod, one of Odin's many sons, offered to take the journey.

Hermod traveled for nine nights until he reached the underworld and met with Hel. He found Baldur sitting next to Hel in the seat of honor. However, he wasn't his cheerful self; he was pale and downcast. Hermod begged Hel to bring his brother back to the land of the living. He told her how all living beings and gods were grieving over Baldur's death. She told him to prove that everyone was indeed mourning him. Hel promised him that if every being in the universe wept for Baldur, she would bring him back to life. However, Baldur would remain in the underworld if one creature didn't.

Hermod carried the message back, and the gods sent word across the cosmos. Everyone and everything wept for Baldur except Tokk, the giantess. You may have guessed it. This wasn't a real giantess, but Loki disguised as one to prevent Baldur from returning. His plan succeeded and Baldur's light was gone forever, condemned to spend eternity in the cold and dark underworld.

What Loki did couldn't go unpunished. He knew the gods were angry and were coming for him. He escaped and shapeshifted into some salmon, but Odin found him and informed the gods of his location. Loki was very intelligent, and the gods struggled to catch him as he kept shapeshifting and hiding in the sea. However, after many failed tries, Thor managed to catch Loki. The gods bound him in a cave and left a serpent above him, dripping venom over his face. Loki's screams were so loud that they shook the earth. He remained in the cave until Ragnarok.

The Myth of Ragnarok

If you watch Marvel movies, this name probably sounds familiar. Ragnarok was featured in one of Thor's movies. Although the story was portrayed in a light tone, the myth behind it is much darker. If the Viking's stories were chapters, the myth of Ragnarok should be the one closing the book since it foretold the end of the universe. The word Ragnarok means "the fate of the gods." The Vikings believed that Ragnarok would happen sometime in the future.

One day, the Norns (female beings who controlled the fate of the gods and mankind and who were even more powerful than all the gods, including Odin) will enforce a great winter. It will be different from any winter the world has ever seen. There will be snow coming from all directions, biting wind, and freezing cold. This winter will be longer than any other winter lasting for about a year without experiencing the warmth of the spring or the summer heat. As a result, the Earth will perish, and people will struggle to find food. They will have no choice but to forgo their morals and break the law to fight for their survival. Families will turn against each other and use their weapons instead of their tongues. Fathers will kill their sons, and brothers will murder each other.

Skoll and Hati, two mythical wolves who spent their time pursuing the sun and the moon, will achieve their goal during Ragnarok and devour the sun and the moon. The stars will also disappear, leaving the skies and the world void and dark. The mighty tree Yggdrasil that holds the cosmos together will tremble and will cause the collapse of all the mountains and the trees. Fenrir, a monstrous wolf and Loki's son (whom the gods have chained), will break free and wreak havoc. His mouth is huge, and he will run around devouring everything and everyone in his way. His brother Jormungandr, the serpent who resides at the bottom of the ocean, will rise and flood the Earth. He will use his venom to poison the Earth's air, land, and water. Then comes Naglfar, which is a ship made from the nails of the dead and whose crew are all giants, and its captain, the god of mischief himself, Loki. According to the myth, Loki will break free from his cave during Ragnarok and join his crew on Naglfar. They will sail and destroy everything in their way.

The sky will split open, paving the way to Muspelheim, a mythical world where giants made of fire reside. Their leader will have swords brighter than the sun. He and his people will come to Asgard through Bitforst (a rainbow bridge guarded by Heimdall. It connects to Midgard, the world where mankind resides). The people of Muspelheim will destroy the bridge. Heimdall will warn the gods that the moment they have been dreading has arrived. The gods are determined to not go down without a fight and will prepare to face the invaders. Their actions show extreme courage and bravery since they know from various prophecies that the battle will not end in their favor.

With the help of the spirits of all the soldiers in Valhalla, Odin will face Fenrir. Odin and his soldiers will fight with everything they have, but, unfortunately, they will be no match to Fenrir, who will devour them all. Odin's son Vidar will go after Fenrir to avenge his father. He will be wearing a shoe that was made for this very moment. Vidar will succeed and kill Fenrir. Loki and Heimdall will fight to the death as both gods will kill each other. Freyr, the god of peace and one of the most beloved gods in Norse mythology, will kill the leader of the Muspelheim. Thor will fight Jormungandr and kill him with his hammer but not before he spits his venom over Thor, leaving him to die moments later. Whatever and whoever is left after this battle will sink into the sea. The world will be empty as if it was never occupied by gods or mankind. To paraphrase the famous words by T.S. Eliot, this is the way the world ends, not with a bang but with Ragnarok.

Although many believed this was the end of this myth, others believed that this was merely the beginning. Not all the gods will fall. Hodr, Vali, Vidar, and Thor's sons Modi and Magni will survive. A man and a woman hidden during Ragnarok will emerge and act as Adam and Eve and populate the world. The sun's daughter will shine and light the skies.

The Myth of Thor's Hammer

If you are interested in comic books and Marvel movies, you are probably curious about the origins of Thor's hammer. Well, this story begins with none other than Loki. Thor was married to the goddess of fertility, Sif, who was famous for her long and beautiful golden hair. One day, Loki felt more mischievous than usual and decided to cut Sif's hair off. Thor fumed with rage, and he captured Loki and told him that he would break every bone in his body. Loki begged Thor to spare his life, and he offered to go to the home of the dwarves to ask them to craft a new head of hair for Sif that would be marvelous and more beautiful than her old hair. Thor agreed to let Loki go, and, for once, he kept his word. He convinced the dwarves to craft a new head of hair for Sif.

Loki decided to stay with the dwarves and caused chaos there as well. He challenged the two to create something unique and better than the other dwarves. He even bet his head that they would not be able to create anything special. Loki shapeshifted into a fly and taunted the two dwarves as they worked. One of the dwarves, Sindri, created a hammer, unlike anything anyone had ever seen. Once thrown, the hammer would always hit its target, never miss, and then fly back to its owner. However, nothing is perfect, and the hammer had one flaw: *its handle was too short.* Sindri named the hammer Mjollnir, which means lightning.

Loki took what the two dwarves crafted, including the hair and Mjollnir, and gave them as gifts to the gods. Sif was the recipient of the hair, and Thor was given Mjollnir. The gods appreciated the gifts but reminded Loki that he lost the bet and therefore owed the dwarves his head. When the dwarves came to collect, Loki, the ever so cunning god, told them that he bet his head and not his neck. The two dwarves then decided to sow Loki's mouth shut.

The Myth of Odin and the Runes

Now we come to the most important legend in this chapter: the runes' discovery. In Norse mythology, the runes are considered the language of the gods. In fact, we can't talk about Norse mythology without mentioning the runes because they played a big role in the mythology.

Odin had always sought knowledge and wisdom. He even sacrificed his eyes to drink water from a well that would grant him knowledge of everything. Before the Latin alphabet became widely used, the Norse and Germanics relied on letters referred to as the runes. However, the runes weren't alphabets like the Latins, but they were symbols. These symbols were very powerful, and Odin was adamant about uncovering their secrets.

The Norns used the runes to shape the fate of the gods and mankind by engraving these symbols on Yggdrasil. Odin wanted this power for himself and wanted to learn about the mysteries of the runes. However, these symbols didn't reveal themselves to anyone unless they deemed themselves worthy of such power. Odin, who never hesitated to make a sacrifice for the sake of knowledge, hung himself from a Yggdrasi's branch and pierced himself with a spear. He remained in this position while looking downward at the water below. He made it clear to all the gods that they shouldn't rescue him. After nine days, the runes finally accepted Odin's sacrifice and began uncovering their mysteries to him. Odin began seeing the symbols of the runes, and all the knowledge behind them was revealed to him. This knowledge made Odin one of the most powerful beings in the universe and allowed him to help himself and his friends and vanquish his enemies.

There is no wonder that Norse mythology is extremely popular to this day. It is filled with fascinating tales about various gods and goddesses. The Vikings humanized their gods by giving them strengths and weaknesses instead of creating a perfect image of the divine. They also experienced human emotions like anger, pain, loss, and envy. With Ragnarok, the story of how the world ends, the Vikings depicted their gods as heroes who were willing to fight even when they knew they would lose and perish. This is quite similar to the traits of the Viking soldiers, who were known to be brave and fierce warriors.

Now that you have become familiar with Norse mythology, you are ready to uncover the secrets behind the runes.

Chapter 2: The History of the Runes

In the previous chapter, we discussed how Odin's thirst for knowledge led him to uncover the secrets of the runes. Odin, one of the most powerful gods in the universe, had to hang himself to appease the Norns so he could uncover the mysteries of the runes. Was his sacrifice necessary? Are the runes that important? What exactly were the runes? These are all the questions we will cover in this chapter.

What Are Runes?

The runes are a reading system but were regarded as *much more*. They were considered a gift from the divine, and indeed they were. Odin sacrificed himself to learn about the runes and give their knowledge to mankind. Although the runes acted as letters the Norse people used to communicate with each other, they were different from the letters we are accustomed to today. A rune is a pictographic symbol of cosmological power. When you write down a rune, you aren't just writing a letter or drawing a symbol; you are invoking the power behind it. The runes gave the Germanic people answers to life's most complicated questions and helped them look at situations from a different and more insightful perspective.

The word rune has a different meaning in many languages. For example, in Old Norse, it means "mysteries," in Old Irish, it means "secret," in Old English, it means "whisper; in Middle Welsh, it means "magic charm," in Finnish, it means "chant" or "song," and in Icelandic, it means "friend." Before the word "runes" referred to the Norse alphabet, it used to mean a "hushed message." Many of these translations are quite appropriate descriptions of the runes since they were, in fact, a secret language until Odin uncovered their secrets.

Unlike how alphabets were written over the centuries using ink and paper, the Norse people carved the runes on hard surfaces like wood, metal, or stone.

The Norse and Germanic people believed that the runes were magic. They even engraved them on their jewelry, weapons, and amulets to give them power. For this reason, they didn't just use the runes as a regular alphabet for writing and communication. Like Odin, they also believed in the metaphysical power behind the runes' symbols. The Norse people took advantage of this power to help them communicate with the supernatural world and incorporated them into different incantations.

Since the runes were considered divine and enchanting, they were connected to the names of various Norse gods. For instance, the rune Thurs is associated with Thor, and the rune Tyr is associated with Tyr, the god of war.

How the Germanic People Used the Runes

It is believed that the Germanic people used the runes from 160 AD to 1500 AD. Instead of using them to simply communicate with one another, the Vikings used the rune symbols according to the powers they invoked. For example, they uncovered their secrets and used them to predict the future, marked their fallen heroes' graves with the runes' symbols, and they also used them to honor their ancestors. There are also rune inscriptions on buildings, bricks, cliff walls, crafts, art, religious objects, magical charms, and weapons.

The boulders the Vikings used to honor their dead are called runestones. There are thousands of rune-stones in Scandinavia, and historians estimate that there are over 3000 of them. The Vikings needed big rocks to commemorate their dead as sometimes they would inscribe a whole poem for them. One of the most popular runestones that featured a poem was the Kjula Runestone which was about the fall of a man called Spear. During the Viking era, the runestones were usually found near graves. They are usually found in

Denmark and Norway, but most are in Sweden.

Although some people believed that the runes could predict the future, others believed that they could give them an idea of what the future held and help them find solutions to their problems. The runes merely offered suggestions of what a person should do in case a certain event took place. Simply put, they gave people hints of how they should act, but the rest was up to them. They were free to make their own decisions or let their intuition guide them.

The Vikings believed in free will, so when the runes suggested something about the future, they didn't treat it as something fixed. They believed that they could change the outcome if they made different decisions. The Norse people appreciated the rune guidance as it helped them see the bigger picture in various situations and provided them with more information to make better decisions.

Later, the Vikings began using the rune alphabets for communications. In fact, we have believed for centuries that the runes were only used on religious objects and to commemorate the dead. However, in the 1950s, excavators discovered in Norway that the Vikings used the runes like regular alphabets for correspondence and business. Just think of how we use letters now. The Vikings used the runes for the same purposes. Whether they wrote jokes, sent love letters, inscribed prayers, or sent personal messages, the runes were a big part of how the Germanic people communicated with each other.

The History of the Runes

The fascination with runes isn't something new. Since they were featured in J.R.R. Tolkien's "Lord of the Rings," people have been curious about them and their origins. The Northern Germanic people were the ones that created the runic symbols in 100 A.D. Historians believe that when the Germanic people raided places near the Mediterranean, they were influenced by the ancient Roman alphabet. However, others argue that they were influenced by the Etruscan letters.

When runes were first discovered, they were only used for inscriptions. Archeologists found runic inscriptions on a Vimose comb in Denmark that they believed to have dated back to 160 A.D. Runes were a huge part of Norse mythology since the Norse people used them to memorialize their main historical events like their wars and stories of their gods.

Although only the Norse and Germanic people used the runes, inscriptions are found in countries like England, Greece, Russia, Greenland, and Turkey. The Viking travelers didn't use any other alphabets, so they would inscribe the runes wherever they went on journeys or when they conquered a new country.

The Vikings used the runes for over 3000 years until the Middle Ages. By then, Latin alphabets were taking over the world, and the use of the runes had died out. However, as mentioned, they are still used in modern literature.

In the 20th century, Nazis started using runes again. They were responsible for spreading confusion and portraying the runes negatively. They believed that the runes were the first alphabet known to man. However, this wasn't true as various cultures had their own alphabets well before the runes came into being. They modified them and started using them, which led to the spread of misinformation surrounding these symbols. For instance, the swastika, considered a sacred symbol during the Viking era, became associated with the Nazis. Luckily, authors like J.R.R. Tolkien and J.K. Rowling gave a new life to the runes and made people curious about their origin so they could discover that they were enchanting symbols that didn't have any evil or racist roots.

The Runes in Literature

We mentioned how Odin wanted the power of the runes all to himself. Indeed, he always sought knowledge and wisdom. However, he was also jealous of the Norns and how they could control everyone's fate by using the power and knowledge of the runes. The story of Odin's jealousy and sacrifice was mentioned in the poem Hávamál, which translates to "Sayings of the High One," referring to Odin. This poem is a part of the Poetic Eddas, which are collections of anonymous Old Norse poems. Still, if it wasn't for Odin's sacrifice, it is believed that mankind would never have been able to learn about the runes or their power and magic. Odin was the one who gave the world the knowledge of the runes. However, he knew how powerful and mighty they were, so he kept some of the most powerful ones to himself and shared the others with mankind. This is another proof of Odin's wisdom as he knew men couldn't handle such power as, in most cases, it would corrupt them.

The runes were heavily featured in literature, especially in poetry. The Norse and Germanics, like many other ancient cultures, didn't record their tales in writing but passed them down orally. Many of the runic poems passed down to us were written after Christianity spread through Europe, and pagan ideas were no longer welcomed. For this reason, the runes went through various interpretations. Small verses in Norse, Icelandic, and Old English literature explain the meaning behind the runes. However, these verses were written after the runic lore was lost, which is why some of these poems seem to contradict each another and can be confusing. Additionally, runes were used in various Scandinavian countries, and we believe that they didn't share the same meanings.

The Runic Alphabets in Germanic Cultures

Although we refer to them as runic alphabets, the runic system is called Futhark runes. This name was chosen to avoid confusion. The word alphabet comes from the words "alpha" and "beta," the first two letters in the Greek alphabet. Unlike the alphabets we use now, the runes didn't start with the letters A and B, which is why the scholars opted for Futhark instead.

Like the Latin alphabet's strong connection with Christianity, nobility, and Catholic scholars, the Futhark runes played a huge role in the Norse religion. They were used in various rituals, and, until this day, runic inscriptions can be found on church walls. Runes and their religious connection should come as no surprise since they were considered divine as they came from Odin.

Several runic letters and inscriptions discovered gave us an idea of how the Germanic people lived their daily lives. For instance, the word "*litiluism*" was found carved on a ship which translates to "man knows little." This can reflect the wisdom of the people back then and how they were aware that they didn't know everything and that there was still much they needed to learn. There was also an inscription found in Gol Stave Church in Norway that says, "*Kyss á mik, þvíat ek erfiða,*" which translates to "kiss me because I am troubled." This saying is believed to refer to a saint who was hung there. There were also rune inscriptions on various things to declare ownership. For instance, women would engrave their names and the runic word for "own" on their buckets.

The Vikings weren't just warriors. Love and romance were a part of their culture as well. Runic alphabets were used to send sweet and romantic messages, albeit using some of the strangest methods. For instance, on the bones of a cow, this sentence was engraved "*kyss mik*," which means "kiss me." On another bone, the words "*Óst min, kyss mik*" were engraved, meaning "my love, kiss me." They also used the rune letters to write love poems, usually inscribed on rune sticks.

Rune letters were also used in businesses. Tradesmen often sent inscribed rune sticks of the merchandise they sent to other merchants. For instance, they would engrave the merchant's name and add the products they were selling, like "Merchant (name) is sending you salt." There were also engravings and short inscriptions on jewelry, especially that worn by dead women. The exact meanings behind these inscriptions remain a mystery as they are hard to translate. However, they may have been the jewelry owners' names or their makers.

The written word has always been associated with news and gossip. Rune letters are no different. Engravings were found that indicate the Germanic people used runes to spread idle gossip. The Vikings also used to engrave their weapons, but there are still debates on what these engravings mean. They are either the names of the weapon's owners or their makers. They could also be the characteristics or the names of the weapon itself. For instance, one of the weapons had the rune word for "black" engraved on it. This could be either the owner's name, the maker, or the weapon's description. There were engravings found on shields as well. These engravings indicate that the soldiers and the silversmith were literate.

There is a misconception among many people that the Vikings didn't know how to read. This is probably the result of how they are usually depicted in movies or TV shows as savages who only care about fighting or conquering other countries. However, from everything we have learned so far and the existence and popularity of the runes back in the day, it is quite obvious that the Vikings were anything but illiterate. They understood and used the runes in their everyday lives. The biggest proof that they could read the runes is the thousands of runestones that were found all over Scandinavia. However, some scholars believed that the Vikings could only read and understand the runes at a basic level. The Vikings believed that only the gods could understand the wisdom behind them.

Although the Germanics used the runes mainly in their Scandinavian language, later, they began using them to write in other languages as well. A few inscriptions were found where the Germanics used the runes to write Latin text, and there were also a couple of occasions where they used the runes to write in English.

Runes in Norse Magic and Divination

During the Viking era, words weren't so easily uttered. One couldn't say a word and then go back on it. Words held extreme power. The way people pronounced each word could directly influence their lives. Once a sentence is spoken out loud, it can greatly impact a person's life. It is out there in the universe, and no power can take it back. Reality can't influence words. In fact, words hold the power to create reality. Words are thoughts. Can you think without using words or language? Languages influence our perception of the world around us. The Vikings believed that once you transformed your thoughts into words, they could, to some degree, alter reality.

Various linguists believe there is a connection between the meaning of a word and the sound it makes. Simply put, the sound carries the word's meaning. The same is applied to the runes, where each word's sound is connected to its meaning. However, as mentioned, runes are symbols, which adds another layer to this theory. There is also a connection between the shape of the rune and the sound it makes.

Therefore, the runes weren't just used to communicate in the physical world. These symbols were powerful enough to be used to communicate with non-human beings and to reach out to the supernatural world as well. For this reason, they can be used while performing magical spells. We mentioned how the Norns used the runes' power to alter the fate of the gods and mankind. Most people use magic to change their fate. They either want to become rich, fall in love, or cure the sick. Magic is all about rewriting one's story so you can change the course of your life.

As a result of its impact on one's fate, the Germanics found that at their core, runes were magic. That said, scholars often have debates on this topic. Some believe that even though rune symbols have been used in various spells, that doesn't mean that they are magical in nature. However, the Vikings may disagree with Egil's Saga, which depicted the life of the Egill Skallagrímsson clan. One day, Egil, a Viking poet, was traveling. He met a Viking farmer who invited Egil to share a meal with him. The farmer had a very sick daughter, so he asked Egil to help him find a remedy for her. As Egil was examining the girl, he found an unexpected surprise. There was a whale bone in the girl's bed with runic inscriptions.

When Egil asked the girl's father about the bone, he told him another farmer's son had engraved these runes; he said the boy was illiterate and most likely had no idea what these inscriptions meant. This was true as the boy only wanted the farmer's daughter to fall in love with him. However, since he didn't understand the meaning behind the symbols, he used the wrong ones and made the girl sick. Unlike the young boy, Egil was an expert. He told the father that these inscriptions were what made his daughter ill. Egil took the bone and destroyed it with fire. He wrote a new inscription using different runes from the ones the young farmer boy used. This was meant to reverse the malice from the whalebone inscriptions. The new runes worked their magic, and the girl recovered quickly. This means that not only were the runes used for spells, but the Nordic people believed the symbols themselves were magic.

This story proves that Norse people believed in the magical powers behind the runes. They understood that these symbols were strong enough to make someone extremely sick and help them easily recover. They didn't just use the runes' magical power in inscriptions. These symbols were also used in various spells and magical formulas. Runes were also used for protection spells, finding love, curing the sick, and everything else. However, one must understand the meaning behind each rune symbol before attempting to use them, or they can backfire, as we have learned from the farmer's daughter's story.

Odin also used the rune magic. He had a spear called Gungnir, engraved with magical runic symbols, and these symbols gave Gungnir magical powers. Just like Thor's hammer, Mjölnir, Gungnir was also crafted by dwarves and could always hit its target without fail.

The Germanic people took advantage of the relationship between the rune meaning and its phonetic sound to perform divination so they could foretell the future. In Norse mythology, practitioners who performed divination were able to foresee the future so they could alter their fate. When Vikings gained experience in using the runes, they used what they learned to practice divination. We understand that the runes were a vital tool the Vikings used in divination. However, we don't know how they used them as this information never got as far as us. Odin's main purpose behind sharing the runes with mankind was magic. He had no interest in people using them for communication.

As mentioned, some believe that the runes aren't magical. They are letters like all the others used in different languages. However, they can still be used in spells. Similar to how we use our alphabet to write or create a spell, the runes can be used in the same way, just like in Harry Potter, where they used the word "Lumos" to light the tip of a wand, using the rune's letters together can create magical words and spells. Runes can be used to create a charm or a spell and engrave it onto an amulet to protect its wearer, heal them, or alter their fate.

For instance, the inscription "healing runes I cut, runes of help" was discovered in Sweden. This charm was used to treat and heal the sick, and it was never specified how they were supposed to heal or what their functions were. The Germanic people clearly believed that the runes were powerful enough and could indeed heal.

To learn about a culture, you should first learn its language. When archaeologists discovered engraved rocks, walls, runestones, etc., they gained insight into the Vikings and learned about different aspects of their lives. This study taught us about the lives of gods, kings, and peasants. The runes and their magical powers made us feel connected with the Nordic people as we can relate to them and their struggles. By learning about the spells they cast, the names of the people they often engraved for various spells, or even the name of the object's makers, we are no longer reading about anonymous people. We are learning about specific individuals with whom we can connect, feel their pain, and sympathize with what they were going through. Runes aren't just powerful because they possess magic and knowledge. They are a language that an entire culture used for 3000 years to create a civilization with fascinating tales and mythology that we are still studying to this day.

Now you have learned about the history of the runes, you are ready to dive in and learn about Elder's Futhark runes and the meaning of each letter in the alphabet.

Chapter 3: The Runic Alphabet

Runes on wood.

https://pixabay.com/images/id-947831/

As you know by now, Odin discovered the runic alphabet after hanging from the Yggdrasil (the World Tree) for nine days. Following this, the runes became available to mankind - beginning with Northern Europe. There is evidence of the runic alphabet on fragments of stone, bark, and bone found in Norse archeological sites - along with other remnants of the ancient Norse culture. With this chapter, you will have a chance to learn how the runes, the archaic Norse language of symbols, make up an alphabet called the Futhark.

While the runic alphabet is rarely used as a language in modern times, learning how to use it even to translate simple texts can help you understand their role in divinations, spellcasting, gridwork, and much more. To help you start your journey, this chapter will also provide tips on how to practice translating texts from modern English to Elder Futhark. In the beginning, it may sound complicated, but after you learn how to write using the runes, you will realize how much they can enhance your practice.

What Is the Runic Alphabet?

The runic alphabet is made up of several runes that create a written language when used together. Several types of runic alphabets are left over from different regions and periods throughout history. The ones that enjoyed widespread and long-standing use include:

- The Elder Futhark (used from the 2nd to the 8th century)
- The Younger Futhark (used from the 8th to the 9th century)
- Anglo-Saxon Futhorc (used from the 5th to 11th century)
- The Medieval Futhark (used from the 12th to the 15th century)
- Dalecarlian runes (used from the 16th to the 19th century)
- Gothic Runes (used from an unknown time to the 4th century)
- Turkic (Orkhon) Script (used from the 8th to the 9th century)
- Old Hungarian Script (used from the 8th to the 11th century)

The oldest one of these is believed to be the Elder Futhark, which is where the name of the runic alphabet (Futhark) comes from. From about 200-800 AD, the Elder Futhark alphabet, a set of 24 runes, was used for writing throughout the Scandinavian region and other parts of Northern Europe. "Futhark" is a word derived from the first six letters of the alphabet, which are "Fehu," "Uruz," "Thurisaz," "Ansuz," "Raidho," and "Kenaz." The 24 letters of the Elder Futhark were divided into three groups called ættir. The first runes of each ættir (Fehu, Hagalaz, and Tiwaz) are also called the Mother Runes because they're believed to be the first runes added to the Elder Futhark alphabet - and all the others in the group - can be tied to them phonetically. This is crucial information as the entire alphabet is based on a phonetic system rather than written forms.

Nowadays, Elder Futhark is typically used to provide background for a better understanding of the Younger Futhark, the alphabet of the Viking Age - which was the successor of the Elder Futhark. Around the end of the 8th century, the Futhark was shortened to 16 runes, and the Younger Futhark was born. The shape of the runic alphabet symbols has also changed. The runic letters have become simpler - with each rune having only one vertical mark called "stave." Vikings found it easier to carve the letters of their new alphabet. They could swiftly move on to more important matters after finishing what they needed to mark down. The runes of the Younger Futhark alphabet are carved with full or long vertical strokes - whereas Elder Futhark often requires three or more strokes per rune.

The Complete List of Elder Futhark Runes

Unlike the letters in modern alphabets, the letters in the runic alphabet have meanings tied to natural forces. And just as nature goes through endless cycles of change, these universal forces also change and evolve with time. And while the runic language doesn't have widespread use nowadays, the meaning of its letters is just as relevant today as they were thousands of years ago. Here is what each rune in the Elder Futhark alphabet means in modern English, alongside their phonetic equivalent and modern pronunciation.

Fehu

- **Symbol:** ᚠ
- **Phonetic Value:** F
- **English Pronunciation:** "FAY-hoo"
- **Translation:** Cattle, prosperity, property, hope, happiness, abundance, wealth, and financial gain.

Uruz

- **Symbol:** ᚢ
- **Phonetic Value:** U
- **English Pronunciation:** "OO-rooz"
- **Translation:** Wild ox, unexpected change, life force, indomitability, strength, power, and good mental and physical health.

Thurisaz

- **Symbol:** ᚦ
- **Phonetic Value:** Th
- **English Pronunciation:** "THUR-ee-sazh"
- **Translation:** Giant, god of Thunder, lightning, thorn, caution, defensive force, and disruption.

Ansuz

- **Symbol:** ᚨ
- **Phonetic Value:** A
- **English Pronunciation:** "AHHN-sooz"
- **Translation:** Wisdom, mouth, listening, breathing, prophecies, communication, and Odin and the ancestral gods.

Raidho

- **Symbol:** ᚱ
- **Phonetic Value:** R
- **English Pronunciation:** "Ra-EED-ho"
- **Translation:** Travel, rest, rhythm, journey, the big picture, change, and momentum.

Kenaz

- **Symbol:** ᚲ
- **Phonetic Value:** C / K
- **English Pronunciation:** "KEN-aahz"
- **Translation:** Controlled energy, torch, fire, passion, light, creation, beacon, and transformation.

Gebo

- **Symbol:** ᚷ
- **Phonetic Value:** G
- **English Pronunciation:** "GHEB-o"
- **Translation:** Gratitude, gift, generosity, exchange, unity, receiving, self-sacrifice, forgiveness, and offering.

Wunjo

- **Symbol:** ᚹ
- **Phonetic Value:** W
- **English Pronunciation:** "WOON-yo"
- **Translation:** Satisfaction, euphoria, fulfillment, well-being, happiness, self-alignment, harmony, and joy.

Haglaz

- **Symbol:** ᚺ
- **Phonetic Value:** H
- **English Pronunciation:** "HA-ga-lahz"
- **Translation:** Hail, destruction, sudden difficulties, violent change of nature, and delay.

Naudiz

- **Symbol:** ᚾ
- **Phonetic Value:** N
- **English Pronunciation:** "NOWD-heez"

- **Translation:** Need, distress, desire for triumph, stagnation, and change manifestation.

Isa

- **Symbol:** ᛁ
- **Phonetic Value:** I
- **English Pronunciation:** "EE-sa"
- **Translation:** Stillness, cold, ice, winter, postponement, delay, and forced pause before a new beginning.

Jera

- **Symbol:** ᛃ
- **Phonetic Value:** J / Y
- **English Pronunciation:** "YAIR-ah"
- **Translation:** Nature's cycle, harvest, rewards for efforts, movement in time, and reaping what you've sown.

Eihwaz

- **Symbol:** ᛇ
- **Phonetic Value:** E / I
- **English Pronunciation:** "EYE-wahz"
- **Translation:** Longevity, wisdom, death, renewal, Yew tree, life, sacrifice, and passing through a gateway.

Perthro

- **Symbol:** ᛈ
- **Phonetic Value:** P
- **English Pronunciation:** "PER-thro"
- **Translation:** Mystery, hidden desires, fate, divination, casting, secret, and the quest for self-knowledge.

Algiz

- **Symbol:** ᛉ
- **Phonetic Value:** Z
- **English Pronunciation:** "Ahl-geez"
- **Translation:** Instinct, sanctuary, elk, luck, connection to the higher self, good omen, and protection.

Sowilo

- **Symbol:** ᛊ
- **Phonetic Value:** S
- **English Pronunciation:** "So-WEE-lo"
- **Translation:** Health, vitality, good energy, enlightenment, spiritual power, success, personal growth, and sun.

Tiwaz

- **Symbol:** ᛏ
- **Phonetic Value:** T
- **English Pronunciation:** "TEE-wahz"
- **Translation:** The God Tyr, victory, bravery, courage, need for justice, honor, and sacrifice for the greater good.

Berkano

- **Symbol:** ᛒ
- **Phonetic Value:** B
- **English Pronunciation:** "BER-kah-no"
- **Translation:** Rebirth, new beginnings, relationship, project, life cycle, and birch tree.

Ehwaz

- **Symbol:** ᛖ
- **Phonetic Value:** E
- **English Pronunciation:** "EH-waz"

- **Translation:** Loyalty, cooperation, movement, forward progress, horse, and partnership.

Mannaz

- **Symbol:** ᛗ
- **Phonetic Value:** M
- **English Pronunciation:** "MAN-naz"
- **Translation:** Balance, intelligence, reason, divine potential, tradition, talent development, and humanity.

Laguz

- **Symbol:** ᛚ
- **Phonetic Value:** L
- **English Pronunciation:** "LAH-good"
- **Translation:** Water, intuition, flow, cleansing, inward journey, personality depth.

Ingwaz

- **Symbol:** ◊
- **Phonetic Value:** Ng
- **English Pronunciation:** "ING-waz"
- **Translation:** Inner growth, male sexuality, potential energy, family lines, perfect timing, ancestry, and fertility.

Dagaz

- **Symbol:** ᛞ
- **Phonetic Value:** D
- **English Pronunciation:** "DAH-gahz"
- **Translation:** The light of the gods, sudden change, awakening, day, enlightenment, inspiration, and self-transformation.

Othala

- **Symbol:** ᛟ
- **Phonetic Value:** O
- **English Pronunciation:** "OH-the-la"
- **Translation:** Spirituality, ancestral property, wisdom, belonging, homecoming, community, and inherent talent.

How Does the Runic Alphabet Compare to Modern Languages?

A phonetically perfect alphabet has a separate symbol (letter or rune) for each sound used in the language. As far as historical evidence shows, the Elder Futhark runic alphabet was like that. We know this because the Proto-Norse alphabet was developed after the Elder Futhark runes, and the former had the exact number of sounds as the former did. However, Roman letters used in the Modern English language are not even close to this ideal phonetic alphabet. There are many sounds without a letter of their own and can be transcribed only through letters or combinations of letters used for other sounds. A great example of this issue would be using sh for (ʃ) or ch for (tʃ).

The following table illustrates how the runic alphabet compares to the modern English, Norwegian, Swedish, and Danish alphabets.

Futhark	English	Norwegian	Swedish	Danish
ᚨ	A	A	A	A
ᛒ	B	B	B	B
ᛞ	D	D	D	D
ᛖ	E	E	E	E
ᚠ	F	F	F	F

ᚷ	G	G	G	G
ᚺ	H	H	H	H
ᛁ	I	I	I	I
ᛃ	J/Y	J	J	J
ᚲ	C/K	K	K	K
ᛚ	L	L	L	L
ᛗ	M	M	M	M
ᚾ	N	N	N	N
ᛟ	O	O	O	O
ᛈ	P	P	P	P
	Q	Q	Q	Q
ᚱ	R	R	R	R
ᛊ	S	S	S	S
ᛏ	T	T	T	T
ᚢ	U	U	U	U
ᚹ	V/W	V	V	V
		W	W	W

		X	X	X
		Y	Y	Y
ᛉ	Z	Z	Z	Z
ᚦ	Th			
ᛇ	E/I			
ᛜ	Ng			
		Æ		Æ
		Ø		Ø
		Å	Å	Å
			Ä	
			Ö	

The runic alphabet is also often compared to the Proto-Norse language - the predecessor of the modern Nordic languages. Some even use Proto-Norse as an intermediary to translate the runic language. However, the phonological system (sound system) of the Proto-Norse language was different from in modern English. For instance, English has the sounds (dʒ), (tʃ), (ʒ), and (ʃ) - which don't exist in the Proto-Norse language. The Proto-Norse phonetic system can't be equated with the Elder Stark alphabet even though it originates from it.

The Anglo-Saxon (the predecessor of the modern English language) script added letters to the runic alphabet to represent sounds of Old English that did not occur in the Elder or Younger Futhark. To start with, Anglo-Saxon Futhark had 28 letters as opposed to the 24 in the Elder one, and after about 900 AD, it already had 33. To this day, Scandinavian languages are even richer in sounds than English. However, instead of adding letters to the Futhark to represent the new sounds, the Anglo-Saxon runic alphabet compounded started to use the same letter to represent more than one sound. For example, they started to use one letter for the phonetic versions of k and g.

In practice, the reduction of the Futhark to 16 letters means that if you don't have the context of the text, it's impossible to tell which sound was meant by a certain rune. On the other hand, as runes became obsolete, the languages were allowed to develop so that the runes were simply reused for a different sound.

Writing Modern Words in Runes

So, as you've seen throughout this chapter, writing modern words using the runic alphabet can be rather challenging. There is no runic outlet designed for contemporary languages - particularly not modern English. Elder Futhark has fewer runes than the 26-letter Roman alphabet used to write modern English. It also has far fewer symbols equivalent to the sounds we use today.

If you try to use the Elder Futhark runes phonetically, that would be substituting runes for the sounds you hear in a word. While the runic alphabet was supposed to be used this way, it won't work with modern English because - as mentioned before- there are not enough runes for all the English sounds. For example, if you would want to spell the word "horse," its rune equivalent as we hear it would be ᚺᛟᚱᛊ, which spells "*hors.*" On the other hand, if you write it as ᚺᛟᚱᛊᛖ, this will change its spelling in the running language. An even more complicated example is the word "knight." According to letters used in English, you would need to transcribe this word as ᚲᚾᛁᚷᚺᛏ, which, to anyone reading it, will sound nothing like the original word. The closest representation of this word phonetically would be ᚾᚨᛁᛏ, which is very different from the way the word is spelled in English.

So, the most convenient solution for transcribing to or from the runic alphabet is to keep the modern English spelling. This would be far easier than figuring out how to combine runes for the letter s and h for (ʃ) when they appear in words like "shame" or c and h for (tʃ) in "child." And it would definitely be a preferable option to dwell on which rune to use when there are 3 variants of the same sound, as is the case with (dʒ) in "joy," "edge," and "gin."

Another curious thing about the runic language is that the same runes were never repeated one after another, even if they appear that way in a word. This is because there weren't too many words like that in the ancient Norse languages. In fact, most of them appeared along with the anglicized version and under the influence of Latin languages. In modern English, for example, the letters c and k often appear one after another. Since the rune for both letters is the same, if you wanted to translate a word containing both, you would only use one rune instead of two. This shortens the word but may take some practice until you learn how to do it correctly because it often leads to confusion when you read it back.

There is also the issue of writing directions. Early evidence shows that there was no set direction to runic writing. Rune carvers would write from left to right or right to left, with some inscriptions combining the two methods. Others even used individual runes written as a mirror image of the main direction of the script. From the archeological evidence from the 11th century onwards, the direction of runic language seems to have been set to the now-familiar left to right. This was probably the result of the influence of Latin languages and is the direction used nowadays to translate modern languages into Elder Futhark runes.

Anglo-Saxon runes are unsuitable for writing Modern English because there are no letters for some sounds that did not exist in Old English. But you can "cheat" and use the late medieval Scandinavian runic alphabet, which has a rune for every letter in the basic Latin alphabet. You can simply substitute a rune for every letter in an English word without caring about the actual pronunciation of the word.

Or you could use runes to write Modern English, partly based on the modern orthography in Latin script but also to some extent on pronunciation. For example, you may use the ng-rune for the sound "ng" in "sing" instead of separating the letters and using the runes for "n" and "g." Typically, someone who wants to write modern English using one of the futharks will replace the English letters in a word with the rune (or combination of runes) that makes the same sound. It can be a little tricky depending on which Futhark is being used, as there isn't a 1:1 correspondence of sounds to characters, but it's usually possible to figure out a way to do it.

Practicing the Runic Alphabet

It's recommended to have the entire runic alphabet and its English equivalents printed or written out on a sheet of paper. Keep this sheet in front of you whenever you practice, thus avoiding wasting time going back and looking up a rune every time you forget which letter it corresponds to. Whether you print it or write it by hand, use block letters for the English as they are closer in their form to Elder Futhark than cursive, which makes them easier to remember.

To avoid any confusion, you should start practicing by translating a few simple English words. Then you can try simple sentences. By mastering them, you may slowly work toward more complicated texts. You can even start by writing your name - beginning with your first name and following up with your last name (and middle name if you have one). That said, even some of the simple names can lead to a bit of confusion when you read them back. If you remember the rule about avoiding repetition, you will understand why this may cause a problem. For instance, if your name is “Jack,” you will write it as ᛃᚨᚲ, and not ᛃᚨᚲᚲ. Remember, when using the runic alphabet, you're not writing the words; you are transcribing their pronunciation.

If you have several repetitions in your name, you may want to start with another word instead. Either way, writing words phonetically will make much more sense for you, at least in the beginning. Here are a few simple sentences you can practice with:

I want to drink water. - ᛁ·ᚹᚨᚾᛏ·ᛏᛟ·ᛞᚱᛁᚾᚲ·ᚹᚨᛏᛖᚱ

The bird sings, and I listen to it. - ᛏᚺᛖ·ᛒᛁᚱᛞ·ᛊᛁᚾᚷᛊ·ᚨᚾᛞ·ᛁ·ᛚᛁᛊᛏᛖᚾ·ᛏᛟ·ᛁᛏ

The air is cold, and the water is frozen. - ᛏᚺᛖ·ᚨᛁᚱ·ᛁᛊ·cᛟᛚᛞ·ᚨᚾᛞ·ᛏᚺᛖ·ᚹᚨᛏᛖᚱ·ᛁᛊ·ᚠᚱᛟᛉᛖᚾ

Use the table above to find the rune equivalent for the letters, write them out, then check if you got them right.

While placing dots between the words is a debated practice, beginners often find it easier to use the dots to separate the symbols. This way, you can ensure that you leave enough room between the words, and you'll be able to read them later without getting confused about which rune belongs to which word. Speaking of reading, this practice should always accompany your writing. Anytime you practice writing a word or sentence, you should also practice reading it back. Move on to a different word only after you are confident in writing and reading the current one.

Having practiced using the simple use of the runic alphabet, you can move on to using bind runes. Bind runes are two runes written on top of each other to make a new one. During the time Elder Futhark was still used, these runes were used to transcribe names, much like the initials we use today. However, you can also use it to empower your magical practice with a rune you designed for that specific purpose. Whether you opt for sticking to the existing runes or creating your own, practicing them is essential to harness their energy. The more you familiarize yourself with each symbol by writing it down, the easier it will be to become connected with their energy.

Chapter 4: The Three Runic Aettir

After reading the previous chapter, you may have noticed that the runes of the Elder Futhark don't follow the same order as the letters of the Roman alphabet. This is because each *aett* is built on a foundation provided by the Mother Runes. These were the first runes of the aett, which were given to mankind by Odin. Every rune that follows them follows logical patterns dictated by the first one. This chapter discusses the three Aettir and their respective runes. It will provide information on the meaning of each aett and runes, as they all form part of life cycles - from birth to death to rebirth. You'll also find a meditation exercise where you can connect with the energy of each aett by focusing on the deities who rule them.

Freyr's Aett

Freyr is the Norse god of fertility who ruled over the first aett. Along with his goddess Freya, this deity represents a unity in which nature, kinships, marriages, and all other relationships prosper. The runes in this aett speak of what you need to achieve to fulfill your destiny. They represent experiences and interactions with your inner self, others, and the divine. They bring order to chaos just as the order was brought on when the universe was created. Freyr's aett contains the oldest runic symbols discovered so far, indicating the beginning of life and the birth of a new culture. From symbolizing survival of this birth to the realization of happiness, these runes empower you in all aspects of life.

Fehu

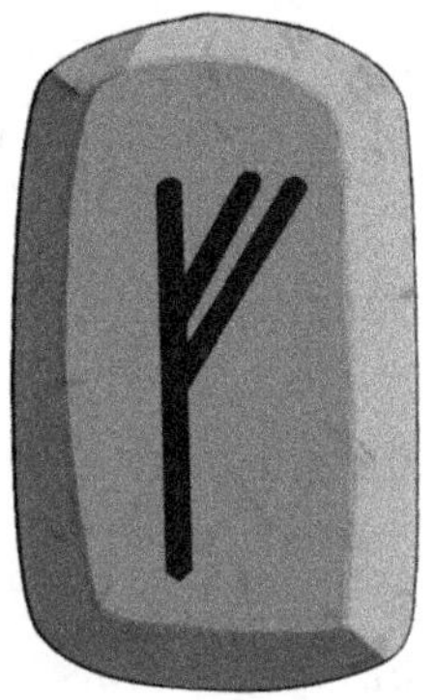

Fehu is a reminder of the present.

https://pixabay.com/images/id-6508602/

Keywords: Prosperity, physical and financial concerns, money, goals, karma, promotion, self-esteem.

Meaning: Fehu is a reminder of our present and the catalyst that awakens a desire to find what lies beyond. It grounds you to your physical location during spiritual journeys and magic acts. It also represents finding what you truly need rather than what you think you desire. Most importantly, Fehu shows that to change your current financial situation, you must first see what changes are possible for you in the future.

Uruz

Keywords: Energy, instinct, vitality, sexuality, wildness, irrationality, fertility, a rite of passage.

Meaning: Uruz represents the acknowledgment of divine forces in nature. Often associated with the god of the sacred hunt, the energy of this rune holds an elemental power that comes from fire. Uruz signals the change from childhood to adulthood and is often used in rituals celebrating this occasion. As the soul within a body matures, it's given a glimpse of the powers of nature.

Thurisaz

Keywords: Hardship, discipline, pain, acknowledgment of inner emotions, awareness of the outside world.

Meaning: Thurisaz depicts an obstacle and foreshadows pain and suffering. However, this suffering is needed to grow and become a stronger version of yourself. What may seem like a huge blow to your ego may be a lesson to push you to make changes happen. Thurisaz tells you that you should allow your destiny to unfold as it should and experience what life has to offer you - good or bad.

Ansuz

Keywords: Leadership, shaman, clairvoyance, the balance of the mind, body, and soul, justice.

Meaning: Representing the ultimate balance, Ansuz signals a point in life where most people choose to remain. When your energies are aligned, you have a sense of fulfillment, and you're tempted to stay in the present. However, Ansuz also points out that you can still make positive changes, further empowering your spiritual and emotional connection with yourself and becoming who you are meant to be.

Raido

Keywords: Change, destiny, journey, fate, progress, progress, life lessons, quest.

Meaning: Raido symbolizes the interwoven twines of fate, representing a web of relationships. Each string is a bond, and every time one crosses another, you gain new connections from the old one. This also means that you can make changes in one relationship without affecting the other ones. Raido shows that you must be aware of all your connections. You can make changes and achieve the desired progress, but your relationships will be affected.

Kenaz

Keywords: Creativity, insight, solution, inspiration, inner wisdom, enlightenment.

Meaning: Kenaz is a rune that brings the obvious solution by giving you subtle messages about the answers you're seeking. While the complete answer may not be revealed to you immediately, this should motivate you to seek the missing parts yourself. Kenaz is the torch that enlightens the path you'll need to follow on your journey and the one that eliminates the darkness surrounding you.

Gebo

Keywords: Gift, generosity, sudden good fortune, relationship, partnership, love, marriage.

Meaning: Often referred to as the rune of connection, Gebo is the first rune that encourages you to break away from the solitary path. It shows you that paying attention to those whose destinies intersect with yours can bring even greater enlightenment. Nurturing your bonds with your loved ones is one of the greatest gifts you can give and receive. It strengthens your relationships and empowers you as a person.

Wunjo

Keywords: Reward, recognition, success, achievement, contentment, fulfillment, joy.

Meaning: As the last rune of the first aett, Wunjo represents the end of a natural cycle and the outset of another. Despite the possibility of a new beginning, you may feel sad that the old has ended, which can leave you stuck in your current position. However, you must realize that your life still holds many lessons, and you must continue your journey. Because the fulfillment you now feel is temporary, and when it passes, you will still feel the need to move on.

Heimdall's Aett

Heimdall is the Norse god of silence and wisdom, known for teaching mankind the universe's rules. He is also said to be a great warrior, often watching out for Loki's malicious tricks and ready to counteract them. The runes of Heimdall's aett warn you about the disruptive forces that cause major shifts in your life. These may change the steady conditions established by the first aett, but you can still make the most of them. The aett helps you navigate the challenging aspects of your life and reminds you that nothing is permanent. The great trials foreshadowed by this aett will forge your character, allowing you to get in touch with your true purpose in life. With their help, you'll learn about the importance of loss and accepting the last phase of a cycle, no matter how painful it may be.

Hagalaz

Keywords: Drastic change, sudden loss, disaster, ordeal, karmic lesson, destruction, clearance, testing.

Meaning: Hagalaz is known to be a harsh wake-up call showing you that you really need to change. Otherwise, you will never achieve happiness.

It's a rather abrupt change after the complacency of the previous rune, especially if you take that for granted. While it's often viewed as a negative sign, it doesn't necessarily have to be. If you choose to embrace the experience instead of refusing to learn your lesson, you can make a difference.

Naudhiz

Keywords: Hardship, poverty, responsibility, obstacle, discontent, frustration.

Meaning: Perhaps to compensate for Hagalaz's hard slap, Naudhiz continues to reinforce the need for change - but more subtly. After communicating with the rune, it often comes as a feeling of discomfort as you realize something isn't as it should be. Naudhiz shows you that if something doesn't go as planned, it means you need to do things differently. Now, you are faced with the dilemma of how to restore the balance between what you want and what you actually *need.*

Isa

Keywords: Stagnation, inactivity, patience, blockage, potential, isolation, reflection.

Meanings: Just as the calm before the storm, Isa represents a period of rest before an abrupt change. It encourages you to take some time to reflect on what you want to achieve and what kind of changes you need. It shows you that although there will always be obstacles, taking the right approach is the key to overcoming them. Isa also allows you to collect your strength so you can face the change when it happens.

Jera

Keywords: Productivity, motion, change, cycle, development, reward.

Meaning: After the period of frozen inactivity granted by Isa comes Jera with the promise of a new beginning. This rune indicates the time for change, growth, and development. You can leave your dissatisfaction behind and enjoy the new flow of positive energy. Your life may not have turned out as planned so far, but this doesn't mean it never will. Jera prompts you to implement your new plans and achieve your dreams.

Eihwaz

Keywords: Initiation, death, change, transformation.

Meanings: Eihwaz marks the turning point in your life's journey by launching you into the transformation phase of the much-needed change. As the symbol of death, Eihway is often viewed as a tool for a passage into maturity and wisdom. Experiencing these changes may be a frightening experience for you, but giving up is not an option. After all, everyone must go through a little suffering before they can reap their spiritual rewards.

Pertho

Keywords: Rebirth, a new beginning, fertility, mystery, divination, sexuality.

Meanings: After accepting the end of a cycle and the abrupt change brought on by the new one, Pertho is there to guide you through the process of rebirth. According to Norse myths, Pertho is the rune that allows you to continue your predestined path through life's perpetual cycles and all the ups and downs. Using this will help you better understand this journey and accept all the changes, whether they are positive or negative.

Algiz

Keywords: Protection, support, assistance, warning, defense.

Meanings: After going through a rebirth, you must face how the changes affect the world around you. Algiz prompts you to use your newfound wisdom wisely to contemplate how your actions reflect on your relationships. It's time to stop focusing on your own spiritual development and see how you can achieve the same. This is another crucial point in life where you must stop and consider your next path.

Sowilu

Keywords: Success, power, positive energy, health, fertility, action.

Meaning: As the last rune in the second aett, Sowilu marks the completion of your individual spiritual journey. Now that you have had time to rest, you'll be ready to launch into action again. The rune encourages you to use the energy you've gathered while resting and move on even if you don't feel the need for it yet. After communicating with this rune, you'll certainly feel the transient nature of your current power.

Tyr's Aett

Tyr is the Norse god of war, also known for his sense of justice and ability to bring order. He is a daring champion who sacrificed his arm to Fenrir so the other deities could trap the giant wolf threatening them all. The runes in Tyr's aett represent a higher spiritual connection, a way to reach the divine forces and seek guidance from them. They allow you to cross that invisible line between the realms and reach out to the divine spirits. At the same time, the runes maintain the connections within human communities, preventing you from losing your sense of humanity. In a way, these rules represent the culmination of all the knowledge acquired from the previous two aettir. They enable you to shift the focus from your individual position and pay attention to the multiple dimensions of your relationships, satisfying nature's laws.

Teiwaz

Keywords: Responsibility, duty, discipline, self-sacrifice, strength, conflict.

Meaning: The first rune of this aett marks a necessary loss brought on by ethical responsibilities. Just as Tyr surrendered his hand in a noble gesture, Teiwaz indicates the sacrifices you'll need to make for the greater good. You can use this rune to tap into the power of its ruling deity and follow up with your duties and responsibilities toward those you encounter on your life's journey.

Berkana

Berkana represents a person who brings positive energy.

https://pixabay.com/images/id-2644529/

Keywords: New beginnings, abundance, fertility, growth, health.

Meaning: Berkana represents the path of a person who brings positive energy into the lives of those around them. Often associated with the birch tree, this symbol is the runic equivalent of spiritual abundance. It helps you heal old wounds and restore frail connections with your loved ones. Berkana also symbolizes fertility in all aspects of life as it fills you with the energy you can use to develop many creative ideas.

Ehwaz

Keywords: Assistance, transportation, energy, motion, hurried decisions, communication.

Meaning: By reminding you that you need to take control, Ehwaz is a rune that promotes balance between all aspects of your life. After gaining all that power, you can't just allow it to roam aimlessly - because if you do, you may end up hurting those around you. To avoid losing the affection of someone, you must listen to the warning of Ehwaz and find the balance and the control you need to navigate your social connections.

Mannaz

Keywords: Family, relationships, community, sense of belonging.

Meaning: Mannaz is the rune that truly puts forward your relationships with your family and friends. It prompts you to form new relationships while nurturing the old ones, satisfying your need for social interaction. However, you must consider how your approach to one relationship affects your other connections. Mannaz will allow you to see all the lives you touch on your journey, teaching you to be more thankful for all the bonds you've formed.

Laguz

Keywords: Fears, negative emotions, secrets, intuition, revelation counseling.

Meaning: Laguz is a rune that'll make you confront your deepest fears regarding your relationships. It encourages you to stop and look at the potential reasons you can't achieve further spiritual development. These reasons are often in our connections with those around us, so by prompting you to help others, this rune can unlock the path toward a higher calling. This will allow you to develop empathy and share your emotions.

Ingwaz

Keywords: Productivity, work, grounding, balance, plenty, nature.

Meaning: For those who long to regain connection with nature, Ingwaz can be a valuable tool. This rune reminds you of our connection with the land, something that's been lost during the industrial revolutions. It can help you find the balance between spirituality and having a productive life without risking getting lost in either of these worlds.

Dagaz

Keywords: Happiness, satisfaction, success, positive activity.

Meanings: Having found the balance between natural life and social interactions, Dagaz will help you reinforce this connection. It acts as a compass, and by following its points, you can find the perfect balance in your life. It reminds you that harmony is possible, which will fill you with a meaningful sense of satisfaction and happiness.

Othila

Keywords: Home, land, property, permanence, belonging, legacy.

Meaning: Othila reminds you that the spiritual wealth you now have access to will surpass the value of the material riches you were promised by Fehu. Whereas physical property was transient, and you were reminded of its possible loss in the second aett, your spiritual legacy will be permanent. This rune marks the end of your journey, where you know who you are destined to be. All the lessons you learned during your travels are now ready to be integrated into your life.

Meditating with the Runes of Each Aett

Like any other form of mindfulness exercise, runic meditation requires physical and mental preparation. Physical preparation means finding a quiet environment where you can focus your mind and won't be disturbed for a couple of minutes. Depending on your practice and preference, it may also involve cleansing your space and body from negative influences.

When it comes to mental preparation, this is usually the first step of the actual meditation, which is done in the following manner:

- Get into a comfortable position. You can sit, stand, or lie down, as long as your back is straight, and you can relax your body.
- Take a few deep breaths to calm your body and stop your racing mind.
- When you feel you can focus on your intention, say a quick prayer to the deity you want to connect with.
- If you are making an offering, too, you can present it right after the prayer.
- Now visualize the rune you want to connect with. If you are addressing more than one, do it slowly and take your time to focus on the image of one before moving on to the next.
- Having formed an image of a rune, exhale deeply and recite the rune name, followed by the phrase representing your intention.
- Inhale again, visualize the next rune, and chant it by drawing it out in your mind and reciting the intention or phrase you want to associate it with.
- If you have trouble focusing on the image of the rune while chanting your intention, feel free to stop reciting and go back to forming the image once again.
- Continue until you've finished with all the runes you want to connect with.
- Return to the present by exhaling slowly and let your mind be filled with thoughts of everyday life.

Ensure the thoughts you address to the runes and the deities ruling the aett they belong to are sincere, positive, and purposeful. You can express your gratitude, seek guidance or peek into the future but only if your intentions have depths to them. You can meditate with more than one rune during one session but keep to the same family. If you seek guidance from more than one deity, you can do it by dedicating a quick session to them on separate days. For example, you can address Frey on Friday, Tyr or Tuesday, Heimdall on Wednesday, etc.

Since the thoughts associated with the runes should be significant for you, it's a good idea to formulate them yourself. Depending on where you currently find yourself in your life's journey and the type of guidance you need, these thoughts can address immediate issues or even long-term goals. Here are a few examples of what you can say when focusing on a run:

- **Fehu:** I know that wealth is power, and I will ward my wealth.
- **Thurisaz:** If I develop my own strength, I know that my power will never fail me.
- **Hagalaz:** The hail of Heimdall is pure, and it will wash away anything bad, revealing the good.
- **Jera:** My achievements will be proportionate to my efforts. The more work I put in, the more rewards I will reap.
- **Tiwaz:** To be happy and successful, I must adhere to order and discipline.
- **Ingwaz:** The key to success is to plan and withhold my power so I can release it at the best possible time.

Chapter 5: The Magic of the Runes and Staves

Historically, runes were used both for writing and for magic. There appears to be a specific power associated with each rune. When combined into magical staves or used alongside spells, runes were used as tools for specific magical purposes, including spiritual transformation and personal growth.

But what is it about the Elder Futhark runes that make them have this kind of mystical power?

Next, we will explore the history of the runes and why they are associated with magic. You will then learn about the magical properties of each rune and how they can be combined to create your own spells and charms.

A Brief Source History of Magical Runes

Runic inscriptions can be found throughout history. There is no defined linear narrative of runes as magical items. Rather, the evidence is scattered along an undefined timeline. This narrative contains inscriptions of historical references, literature, and mysterious carvings such as magical charms and phrases.

Historic Literature about Magical Runes

The Poetic Edda is an untitled collection of Old Norse narrative poetry found in the Codex Regius written during the late 1200s. It contains numerous sources of runic magic. One of the best sources is the Sigrdrífumál, a poem that contains verses detailing how a Valkyrie blessed a hero with the knowledge of runes. Among the other works in this collection, there are poems and stanzas about runes that tell how they are used in spells being taught among the characters mentioned. There is talk of casting a charm spell with the "gladness rune" and other rune names. In all instances, the runes are used for actual magic and ability-enhancing spells.

Besides literature, the runes also appear in numerous Norse myths. Among them, the Norse myth of Odin and the World Tree is credited with inspiring Elder Futhark's runic system. A description of this can be found in the Poetic Edda's Havamàl. The tale of Odin and Loki creating a magical spear with the help of runes so it would never miss its target is one of the most famous tales.

Historical Evidence of Magical Runes

Protective inscriptions and "alu" rune words were discovered during the Roman and Germanic Iron Ages. Carved into spears, shafts, and even bone, these inscriptions appear to have been proliferated by an Erilaz, translated into "runemaster" or "magician."

It has also been documented that charms and spells were made using runes as early as 98AD. Roman politician and historian Publius Cornelius Tacitus, widely regarded as one of the greatest Roman historians by modern scholars, described magical methods and their strict adherence. He mentioned what appears to be spell casting using signs together with natural objects like tree bark and white cloth. He then described the careful inspection and reverence of these signs. This practice appears to be widespread among the community, with family and the state priest in attendance. While the term "signs" is often disputed, it is generally accepted that this refers to written documentation of magical runes in practice.

Historical Evidence of the Magical Purpose of Runes

The Kingmoor Ring, among others, bears runic inscriptions of apparent magical significance. And two runestones in Sweden contain the phrase "runes of power" inscribed upon them.

The Glavendrup stone is a runestone found in Denmark and dates from the early 10th century. It contains a warning curse inscription carved on the stone.

What Makes Runes Magical?

Now that we know some of the historical references to the runes' magical properties, let's look at *how* they were used.

Having discussed the history of the runes in previous chapters, we know they form the Elder Futhark alphabet, a sequence of 24 letters meaning "secret" or "mystery" in the Gothic language. The Germanic peoples of Northern Europe used them for divination, magic, and as powerful talismans and protective amulets in ancient times.

The Norse and other Northern European people didn't use the rune letters for communication and trade. Instead, they marked graves, honored ancestors, and predicted the future with them. They represented great mysteries, morality, and divination. Runes stones were thought to emanate powerful magical properties and were highly venerated due to their historical narrative and so were taken very seriously.

Besides serving as a symbol of cosmic conditions and reverence for higher powers, the runes also served a ritual purpose. The runes influenced every aspect of life, from the sacred to the practical. Health and love were controlled by spells and runes, as were crops, the sea, and the weather. There were runes for death and birth, fertility, and spells to end curses. They decorated houses for safe keeping and Viking ships for protection and strength. Runes were also carved on weapons, food platters, and jewelry.

Elder Futhark Runes- Magical Meaning

Below is a quick reference list of magical and divinatory meanings. This list is not exhaustive, and some meanings overlap.

Rune	Magical Uses
ᛟ OTHALA / O	Influence over possessions, inheritance, experience, ancestry, heritage, and value.

ᛚ LAGUZ / L	Stabilize emotions and turmoil, enhance psychic abilities, uncover the truth, and confront fears.
ᛗ EHWAZ / E	Energy, power, trust, progress, communication, progress, change, transportation.
ᛏ TIWAZ / T	Victory, protection, reinforce will, strength, healing a wound, analysis.
ᛉ ALGIZ / Z	Channeling energy, a shield, Protection, ward against evil, guardian.
ᛇ EIHWAZ / E / I	To ease a life transition, defense, transformation, protection, cause change.
ᛁ ISA / I	Reinforcement of other magics, ice, obstacles, blockages, freezing, and reflection.
ᚺ HAGALAZ / H	Destructive, dangerous weather, breaking destructive patterns, the wrath of nature, uncontrolled forces.
ᚷ GEBO / G	Balance, luck, fertility, successful partnering, giving.

ᚱ RAIDHO / R	Bring about change, protection for travelers, rhythm, facilitate change, and reconnection.
ᚦ THURISAZ / TH	Focus on getting rid of the negative, regeneration, concentration, and self-discipline.
ᚠ FEHU / F	Achieve goals, luck, new beginnings, abundance, success, luck.
ᛞ DAGAZ / D	Clarity, positivity, awakening, awareness, transformation.
ᛝ INGWAZ / NG	Strength, growth, health, balance, grounded, connect.
ᛗ MANNAZ / M	Order in life, intelligence, thought, ability, skill, create.
ᛒ BERKANA / B	Start again, encouragement, desire, healing, regeneration, liberation.
ᛊ SOWILO / S	Cosmic force, energy, healing, strength, cleansing, success.
ᛈ PERTHRO / P	Knowledge of secrets, fertility, enhance the self and powers, control uncertainty.

ᛃ JERA / J/ Y	Fruition, eliminate stagnation, growth, harvest, create change.
ᚾ NAUTHIZ / N	Survival, frustration, endurance, obstacles, determination.
ᚹ WUNJO / W	Happiness, harmony, joy, prosperity, success, motivation.
ᚲ KENAZ / C/ K	Light, motivation, regeneration, inspiration, regeneration.
ᚨ ANSUZ / A	Leadership, communication, wisdom, signals, health.
ᚢ URUZ / U	Understanding, strength, speed, energy, courage, dedication, vitality.

No matter the level of knowledge you have of the Elder Futhark alphabet or where you are at in your learning process, having a guide with each rune name and magical meaning is always helpful.

How Are Runes Used in Spells?

Technically speaking, there is no way to know how our ancestors cast spells with runes. There is, however, some evidence of spell casting through speech, singing, and writing.

There are generally two ways to cast spells with runes. Either write it down and place it with the runes on a cloth, mat, or bowl- known as a talisman. The talisman then transmits its power to your writing. Or cast the spell through speech or chant- known as incantations. In his book "Futhark: A Handbook of Rune Magic," Edred Thorsson devised a specific chant for each rune to create a mantra. But you can do it any way you want.

How Can Runes Be Used to Perform Magic?

Runes could also be used to perform divination. They help manifest intent into physical manifestation by interacting with internal and external energies.

When placing your runes on your item and writing or carving them, a fluid is placed over them. The most common bodily fluids are blood or spit. The runes are typically stained red by alcohol or red dye (blood symbolism). Then, either the rune's name or a short incantation of your choice may be used. A spell may need to be carried or placed near the target of the spell, depending on where it will exert its influence.

Combine Runes to Make Powerful Charms

Between the 15th and 19th centuries, magical charms/staves were found according to Icelandic literature. Staves are made when you combine rune symbols to create an even more powerful magical effect. They were carved into stone, wood, or paper and carried around or placed in the homestead or on ships for protection. An individual's connection with the rune is strengthened when runes are carved manually.

Vikings believed that, when correctly used, runes could manifest ideas.

Vegvísir Viking Stave

Among the most popular staves is the Viking Vegvísir. A magic stave is meant to guide its bearer through rough weather. A map depicting a Vegvísir, which means "that which shows the way," was compiled by Geir Vigfusson in the 19th century. Instead of the round symbol used today, the Huld Manuscript uses a square symbol with eight staves, each ending with a different symbol. Some speculate that each rune symbol represented a direction point, similar to a compass.

The Helm of Awe Stave

The Helm of Awe stave is one of the most recognizable Icelandic symbols, and it is said to provide protection and strength in the battle for anyone wearing it.

There is a strong connection between the Helm of Awe and the runes because some of the shapes on the stave are similar to runes. It is highly unlikely that this correspondence was just a coincidence, given how central the runes were to Germanic magic. The stave used various rune symbols, including the Algiz (Z) rune. Considering this is a rune for strength and protection, it makes sense that it would be used in their stave. It also uses the Isa (I) rune meaning blockage of obstacles.

Rune Spells

Not only was it possible to use runes for divination, but it was also used to obtain desired results. In times of desire, people drew or carved on wood and stone corresponding to runic characters and kept them with them at all times as a reminder of their wishes and desires. Wishes that came true due to runic spells would be burned in open flames once the scripts had worked.

It can be a bit confusing when you're just starting out with Rune Magic to figure out how to perform spells. Here is a simple, step-by-step beginner spell.

How to Make a Spell with Runes

Studying the runes and understanding their meanings first is the most critical step in this process. The final spell could have a different outcome that might affect its general purpose, so you must be careful about what runes you mix together.

Consequently, don't let this prospect put you off. Practicing as much as possible is the best way to learn! Take a look at some of the spells others are doing, and analyze them until you become more knowledgeable on spell making.

1. This is about what you want to achieve with this spell. Use the above chart that describes each rune and its magical properties.
2. After you have looked at the runes, take some time to visualize what you want from this spell. Do you want to be happy and prosper? Imagine yourself in a serene meadow of golden sunflowers.

3. To really make your spell power, you should carefully consider the runes. Think about the meaning and symbolism behind each of the runes. You may find that one or two pop out at you without warning - as if they're waiting for you.
4. To start, only pick 2 runes. You don't want to overcomplicate things when you're just starting out. Take things slowly until you get the hang of it. It is also a good idea to take special care when combining the runes. Working with runes isn't as simple as it seems, and some of them have different meanings than you may think. Make sure you do a lot of research into the history of each rune to select the right one for your purpose.
5. Creating your design is now the next step. We are looking at binding the runes for this spell to create an extra powerful effect. You'll need some paper and a pen. Don't overthink this step. Let your thoughts loose and just go with the flow. The less time you spend thinking about it, the more your inner desire will emerge. Start drawing as much fusing of the symbols as you wish. Feel free to let your imagination run wild and draw whatever comes to mind.
6. Let the drawing settle for a few minutes once you've completed it.
7. Now, take a look at your drawings and choose the one that speaks to you - whichever seems to pop out of the page.
8. Next, pick any material to bind the runes together. If you're casting a self-purpose spell, you will have to carry it around with you. So, choose something practical like stone, fabric, or wood - or turn it into a decoration, frame it, and hang it on your bedroom wall. If the spell is only for a short time, then a piece of paper will usually do the trick.
9. Now, it's time to create the ritual. You know what you want to create your spell, you have chosen the runes to enact it, plus you have your materials ready and waiting. Now, charge your charm with energy and power.
10. Do this next step in any way you want. Some people like to light candles and go into a meditative trance or somewhere quiet away from the outside world. As you draw or carve your rune, it is vital that you keep your purpose in mind.

11. The most important thing is to remain present and in the moment, without losing track of the task at hand, and carve out each of the runes of the bind rune one by one until you have completed the final design of the rune. Take a moment to think about what the meaning of each rune is and how it will help you.
12. Some people like to take a moment afterward to really soak up the event. Again, always remain aware of the purpose of your spell and what you want to achieve from it. Manifestation of desires is one of the main concepts of the runes, after all. Make sure you stay in your thoughts while holding the charm tightly in your hands.

Well done! You have now created your very first rune bind, and it's time to use it. It's not as difficult as you may think to recall the magic of runes. All you have to do to ensure it works is to keep it on or around you until it does its job. Keep it in your bag when you go to work. In addition, if you use more than one bag, for example, at the gym, make sure you swap the charm into the other bag. Put it somewhere you won't forget about it, like in your bedroom.

To maintain the spell's intention, keep it with you at all times.

You can dispose of your bind rune as soon as you achieve your goal. Naturally, this depends on the binding source you used during the spell. If you used wood or stone, it's perfectly fine for you to bury it. A charm can be buried in a place that holds special meaning for some people. If you use paper, you can simply burn it by dropping it into an open flame or lighting it with a candle.

Originally, runes were designed to be used as letters in a language. However, they were much more than letters. By writing or engraving a runic symbol, one invoked and directed the force represented by it. The runes symbolize a meaningful exchange between us and the invisible world. They represent a powerful history that brings people together with nature and the universe.

Chapter 6: Creating and Activating Your Runes

We've already explained the history of the magical properties of the Elder Futhark runes and how they were used as an ancient form of prophecy by those seeking advice.

Now, we will discuss the activation methods in relation to your charm through charging and meditative techniques. If you want your runes to speak to you, they need to be activated. We will then go on to how you can create your very own divination set and how to activate it.

The rune needs to be activated to work.
https://unsplash.com/photos/cBkHr5RuooA

Activating Your Rune Charm

If you followed the guide to making your own rune charm in chapter 5, we will now go a little deeper into how to *activate it.* Knowing how to activate your rune for various purposes is a great skill to have. It is also fun to learn all the different techniques you will be able to add to your divination arsenal.

We will provide you with two activation techniques. The first will rely on a meditative technique using the power of the North Star, also known as Odin's Eye. The other activation technique will involve the properties of Galdr and the ancient form of magical chanting.

Odin's Eye Activation

Sprinkle salt on your charm before charging it and leave it overnight. Salt acts as a cleansing tool, and it also offers protective powers.

Tools:

- Rune charm
- Smoke from herbs/candles
- Compass
- White cloth
- Quiet room
- Table
- Incense

Instructions:

1. Find a quiet spot in your home.
2. Cover the table with your cloth
3. In the center of the table, place the herbs or candle and the incense.
4. Place your charm next to them.
5. Imagine that your charm is the essence of life and that its essence is meant to create a richer, more fulfilling life for you. Then spend a few minutes reflecting on the meaning of your charm.

6. Using the compass, locate North and position yourself and the table facing it.
7. Keeping your eyes closed, place the charm into the palm of your hands, or hover your hand palms over the charm.
8. Put yourself in a meditative state and imagine that the brightness of the Northern Star is pulling you as you meditate. As you get closer, and the light gets brighter, return with the light back through the night sky and into your room. Feel the power of the star flowing through you as you center its energy into your body and mind.
9. Hold the charm up toward the North, thinking deeply about the intention of the charm. Imagine the energy of Odin and the star's energy settling into the charm.

Your charm is now activated.

Galdr Activation

Take note of the names of the runes you used in your charm. We will take the first two or three letters on the runes and combine them to make your Galdr chant. For example, if you used the Ansuz (A) and Dagaz (D) charm to bind the two magical elements together, then your chant could be "An-Dag," "Dag-An," Ans- Da," Da- Ans," "Ans-Dag," or "Dag-Ans." Whichever combination you choose will be just as effective as any other.

Then, when you want to activate your rune charm, you can sit and chant this Galdr while using it in your ritual.

What Can Runes Be Used For?

Did you know that runes can be used for other things besides creating charms and casting spells? They can be used in the art of divination too. First, ask yourself why you want to create your own rune set in the first place. Runes can provide guidance and insight into how things may turn out. They don't act as a fortune-telling tool per se, nor can they offer you solid advice or answers. They can offer insight into your unique situation, which can, in turn, provide you with correct reactionary awareness.

Runic readers recognize that the future isn't predetermined and that individuals can make their own choices. Because of this, you are more than welcome to change the direction if you don't like what you get from a rune reading.

There are many situations where runes can be used. Consulting the runes can be helpful when you have limited information or cannot see the whole picture.

How Does Rune Divination Work?

Remember when you were introduced to casting your first spell in chapter 5? Throughout the process, we stressed the importance of keeping your objective in mind. This is because runes focus on your conscious and subconscious mind when you ask a question or think about an issue. A rune is not entirely random when it is cast in front of you but rather a choice made by your subconscious.

It is common to use runes for divination. Most modern-day users will utilize them to seek answers or even achieve success. In most respects, contemporary runes differ from Elder Futhark runes in that they are far more related to 21st-century questions like inner peace and prayer. You will still be able to interpret your runes easily even though they will possess the same qualities as those used in ancient times.

What Sort of Runes Do I Need for Divination?

Various materials can be used to make runes, including stone, wood, clay, metal, pebbles, bones, and crystals. If you're just starting out and you're trying to find out if you enjoy rune casting, then a simple rune set will be more than enough.

However, once you've practiced for a while and have developed a passion for runes, you'll probably want to have a *divination set* made up of quartz or crystals. These types of sets can be purchased and will usually come with an instruction leaflet on how to use and interpret them.

But, if the runes' history and origin resonated with you, you will probably understand the importance of making your own runes and divination set. Not only does this help you more to understand the concept of runes, but it will bring you closer to them. If they're carved with care and attention, they will be formed as a part of you. Therefore, they will be more likely to understand your energy and provide a more personal insight into your questions and problems. No matter what the material is, it's the way you use the runes that matters most, not what the runes look like.

Rune Divination Set

Just a quick note about the number of runes you need to create. A runic alphabet consists of 24 letters, and the Elder Futhark is the most common for rune divination. This is the set you will be using as inspiration when making yours. Some rune sets include a blank rune, referred to as Odin's rune or Wyrd rune. Some people accept this blank rune as the unknown aspect of fate, while others believe there is no historical evidence that this rune ever existed when the Elder Futhark letters were created. Nonetheless, it is up to you if you want to include it in your divination set. If you do, you will create 25 runes instead of just 24. However, if this is your first time making a set, you may want to make more and err on the side of caution. This way, if you make a mistake during the carving process, you can pick a spare rune without making another one.

It is essential to keep your divination set simple when making your first one. Start by thinking of health, success, strength, and other intents you would frequently use with your runes. You will become more familiar with your runes and will be more sincere about their creation as you spend more time crafting them. Since you've spent a lot of time creating them, charging them will be easier when the time comes. Make each one as significant as the last. We will get into charging them later on.

How to Create Your Own Rune Divination Set

The most common traditional materials for runes were stone or wood. This was because they were simple enough to carve lines into. These days though, we have much better access to molding materials. So, for this divination set, we will use polymer sculpting clay that hardens in the oven because it is easy to find and use. Plus, it is non-toxic and won't make a mess while you're using it.

Tools:

- Polymer clay
- Spatula
- Pencil
- Small carving tool
- Oven set to 110 degrees Celsius/230 degrees Fahrenheit

- Foil or baking sheet
- Black acrylic paint
- Thin paint brush
- A damp cloth or wet wipe
- Clear casting resin

Instructions:

1. Roll some small balls of clay in between your hands (24 for the Elder Futhark alphabet, 25 if you want to include the blank rune. Or more if you want to have spares just in case you make any mistakes during carving).
2. Flatten them out using a spatula to avoid fingerprints. Not too thick, around 0.5 cm / 0.19 inches.
3. You can make them into any size you want- big or small, it's up to you. This is an advantage of making your own.
4. This next step is optional, but we will make the runes into charms for duality too. So, take a pencil or something sharp with a tip, and poke a hole through the top of each piece of flattened clay. This way, you can use the runes as charms and wear them as a necklace.
5. Now, we will carve the rune letters into the clay pieces. You can use a pencil or a small clay spatula.
6. Carve each symbol into the rune about 1- 2 mm in depth. This way, the symbols will be clear when baked.
7. Take your time when carving the symbols, and remember if you want to use them as charms, then keep the hole for the charm at the top.
8. After you have finished carving, place your clay pieces onto a foil or baking sheet and onto a baking tray.
9. Place them into the oven at around 110 degrees Celsius / 230 degrees Fahrenheit and bake them for around 30 minutes.
10. After 30 minutes, the clay pieces will be hardened. Leave them to cool for another 30 minutes.
11. This next step is optional, but it does help to make the symbols stand out more. Take your black acrylic paint and brush and carefully paint into the indents of the rune carvings.

12. After painting each rune symbol, things may look a little messy. If so, take a damp cloth and carefully wipe away any residue. This step won't rub the paint away as the carvings will be deep enough to hold the paint inside rather than outside.
13. Leave the paint to dry.
14. To keep your runes from wear and tear (and looking nice and sturdy), paint the runes with a clear resin. This will give them a nice shine. Again, leave the resin to dry.

And there you have it. Your very own divination set is carved and created with care and attention.

Activating Your Divination Set

When we say activating, we mean charging the set with energy. This doesn't necessarily mean charging them with the power of a full moon but instead igniting them with your spirit and trust.

Runes are a tool for divination, but their interpretation relies on the human essence within each individual. Therefore, every divination practice begins with some form of ritual designed to quieten the mind and reconnect the reader with their intuition.

The next step is to put your question out into the universe, again using your mind's power. The Vikings believed that all natural forces in the world were interconnected. In other words, if you ask a question with intent, the historical forces that were so revered by the ancient use of runes can help you find an answer.

For the activation to be a success, there is, however, one thing to note before you start. During activation, you must know the meaning of each of the runes. This will ensure you initiate the correct essence of the rune meaning.

Some people choose to use tag locks in this part of the activation ritual. This means the use of bodily fluids like blood or spit. But if you're not comfortable with using bodily fluids, you can still activate the runes with the same connection by following these steps.

1. For those interested in using a tag lock with their runes, you need to dab each of the runes with a little of your blood or saliva as you follow the steps below. If you're not interested in locking any bodily fluids into the runes (it's not absolutely necessary, and we don't want you to hurt yourself!), then by all

means, skip this step.

2. Take each of your runes, one by one, and either place it against your forehead, over your heart, or hold it between the palms of your hands.
3. Actively visualize it in your mind as you do this. Try getting into a meditative stance or prayer if possible.
4. When you feel you're ready, go ahead and dab a little bit of your blood or saliva onto the carving of the rune. As you're doing this, keep saying or chanting the name of the rune.

   Runecasters use this step as a way to create a link and hear the rune speak to them, not necessarily with words, as it is more of a feeling.
5. Again, hold the rune against your forehead, heart, or in between the palms of your hands and give it just a moment to charge.

During this step, some prefer to say a specific chant, breathe onto the rune, or say "so mote it be" or "thank you." This can create a bond between you and each of the runes. Remember, there are 24 runes to a set, so you will have to do this activation step at least 24 times. For those who dabbed their runes with fluids, you can add a sealant over them to keep them from chipping away.

Once you have activated the runes and this step is complete, you can cast the runes. They can be thrown down, drawn from a bag, or used in any other way. A rune's position in relation to each other and where it falls will determine how the answer is interpreted.

We will discuss exactly how to read the runes you cast in another chapter. But for now, know that researchers and mystics have developed several different ways to read the runes for divination, and there is a wide range of approaches. Nonetheless, you will discover that every practice relies on connecting with your intuition through the runes.

Taking Care of Your Runes

Cleansing and activating your runes is an integral part of caring for them. Providing you treat runes with respect, they can become a powerful supportive tool. How often you perform your cleansing rituals will depend on a few factors, but essentially it is up to you how often you recharge them. If the runes are new or have been touched by other people, then it makes sense to reactivate their power for them to bind to you and only you. Runes should be kept as close to you as possible since they are often considered personal items. Tuning into your own energy by keeping them close to you at work or in your bedroom will help you receive a more accurate reading.

You can keep your runes in a pouch to keep them safe.
https://unsplash.com/photos/vzrKcFry8Sc

Runes can be stored in a box, or a bag made of natural materials. In addition to velvet pouches, some prefer wooden boxes with a selenite stick inside. Selenite is a natural healing crystal, so its properties can emit powerful healing energy to your runes.

You should always remain emotionally centered no matter how you activate your rune charms or divination set. It is possible for the higher forces that you call upon to have either a positive or negative reaction to your questions, depending on your inner feelings during the ritual.

By now, you should have a better understanding of what it takes to call on the magic of the Elder Futhark runes. Once you are familiar with their meaning, the next step will be for you to activate your rune charms. Once you have done that, the process should energize your creative subconscious into making your own divination set.

Chapter 7: Seiðr: The Art of Runic Divination

In this chapter, you'll learn to develop the ability of Seiðr - the practice of predicting the unknown by reading the Elder Futhark runes. To start with, you'll be given a comprehensive insight into divination in general and Seiðr as a practice and the results you can expect from it. Like any other divination practice, Seiðr requires you to prepare your space, some tools, your body, and your mind. Having gone through these elements, you'll be ready to move on to the topic of rune casting and learn how to use runic spreads as a form of guidance to address current problems or situations. You'll also be provided with a quick recap of the meaning of each runic symbol to help you read them and find the answers you seek.

Divination and Seiðr Basics

Divination is a method of tapping into your intuition to access knowledge hidden from your conscious thought processes. Your subconscious mind communicates what it sees and interprets as spiritual messages, allowing your conscious mind to decipher them. Several forms of divination include dream interpretation, scrying with crystals, using Tarot cards, coins, and tea leaves, and casting runes. Divination through runes is very similar to reading Tarot cards in that it won't help you predict the future. It's a guidance tool that works with your subconscious to solve problems or overcome situations by looking at potential outcomes.

Seiðr is a type of Norse magic related to telling and shaping the future. According to Norse myths, Seiðr was primarily associated with the deities Odin and Freya, who then taught the practice to the other Norse Deities. Later, the practice was passed on to mankind in general and was said to be reserved for the females of each generation. Nowadays, practitioners of Norse Magic still use Seiðr as a reliable divinatory practice.

To perform Seiðr, a practitioner must enter a trance to interact with the divine forces. Then, they ask questions related to prophesy or guidance for future actions. The Seiðr rituals may be performed to seek out hidden knowledge - whether it's hidden in a physical location or in your mind, attracting good luck and many other attainable purposes. In ancient times, they were also done to heal the sick, control the weather, settle disputes, and bring the opposite of all the above. However, since the method revolves around questions from the past, present, and future, casting and consistently interpreting runes is nearly impossible. The only way to practice Seiðr divination reliably is to use it for attainable, conscious goals.

What You Need for Practicing Divination

The first thing you'll need to practice runic divination is a set of runes. Here, you can either buy a set of pre-made runes or make your own, as many practitioners of Norse Paganism do. While the first is probably easier for newbies, making runes enhances your connection with them, which makes them work even better for you. If you go for the first option, you can choose between runes made from stone, wood, and crystals. Carving runes into crystals infuses them with an added element called natural vibrations, which can be used for various purposes.

If you choose to create your own runes, you can inscribe them into pieces of stones or nut-bearing wood, like hazel, oat, pine, or even cedar. Apart from carving, you can also paint the symbols with acrylic paint (highly recommended for beginners) or burn them into the wood (only recommended if you have experience using burning tools). Carving your own runes can be part of the magical preparation process for any spell, divination, or other magical act. It can be beneficial for your practice, but it shouldn't be taken lightly; otherwise, you'll miss out on infusing your runes with your powers.

You'll also need to prepare a surface to work on. This can be your altar or any other sacred space you usually practice in. If you are going for the cloth method, you will need to lay a piece of fabric on your prepared surface. You may use any type of incense, candles, oils, crystals, or any other tools that help you get into the right frame of mind to access the information you seek. Apart from these items and the runes, you may prepare symbols of the guide you are working with. If you are seeking divinatory guidance from a Norse deity, you should have something that symbolizes them. This can be a picture, an object, or the drawing of the rune that represents them.

Runecasting

Runecasting is a popular oracular divination method used by practitioners of Norse magic. It involves casting runes to receive guidance to handle problems or situations that you need help with. Runecasting is essentially very similar to Tarot spreads or pulls, as it also offers a better perspective for a variety of situations - some general, others more specific. The latter is a more common purpose, as you have better chances of receiving an answer to a concrete question rather than a generic one.

Each rune of the Elder Futhark has a corresponding meaning, and the ones laid out in front of you will guide you toward possible answers or solutions. That said, just like with any divination method, runes won't give you the exact answer to your questions, nor do they offer direct advice on what you should or shouldn't do with your life. Instead, they suggest different outcomes and factors that may influence these. Runecasting can be a great tool to enhance your intuition and learn to rely on it by applying some critical thinking skills. Like with Tarot spreads, the rules don't reveal anything fixed. Your actions can influence the outcome of different situations and drastically alter them. So, if you don't like an outcome, change what you are currently doing, and the results will be more to your liking.

How to Cast Runes

According to Norse traditions, the runes are cast on white cloth. This provides a neutral background so the caster can focus on the results. The color white is also considered magical and is believed to enhance the forming of the magical bond between the runes and the person casting them. While there are practitioners who prefer casting onto the ground for better access to natural magic, the choice will be up to you.

Some runecasting methods involve tossing the runes in front of you - others will require you to lay them out in an elaborate pattern. With the first ones, you can also choose between keeping your eyes closed or open while looking at the sky during casting. When the runes land, you can open your eyes/lower your head and read them. Casting a runic spread is similar to laying out a Tarot spread. You hold the bag or box in your hand, formulate your questions, and start pulling out the runes one by one. You place them in the shape of the spread you've chosen to interpret.

Whichever method you choose, keep your runes in a bag or box until you are ready to cast them to prevent them from getting infused with negative influences. Before you start the divination process, prepare your space by cleansing it, and you can do the same with your mind and body too. Make sure you have the right questions and intentions in mind by considering your current situation and what you want to achieve in the future. You may even do a meditation exercise preparing your mind to focus or say a quick prayer to the deity you are asking for assistance.

How to Use Runic Divination Spreads

There are a few different layouts that can help you tap into your intuition and reveal the answers to the questions you ask during your divinatory practice. The simplest one is the 1-rune pull, although this isn't truly adequate for divination because it only answers yes or no questions. That said, it can still be great for practice and learning the meanings of the runes, especially if you are familiar with the Tarot, as this is very similar to the daily 1-card reading method. It involves pulling one rune out of your bag and looking at it to interpret its meaning.

You'll need more runes to get information about past and present influences and future outcomes. Popular spreads involving multiple runes are the 3-rune layout, the 5-rune layout, the 7-rune layout, the 9-rune layout, and the 24-rune layout. Before you cast any of the spreads, you should put your hand in the bag you keep your runes in.

Move your hands around to shuffle the runes before spreading them. Since runecasting typically addresses a particular issue, you should consider which problem you want to explore. This will help you access the influences of the past and present.

The 3-Rune Layout

This is one of the most ancient layouts, as traditionally, the Norse cast their runes in 3, or multiples of 3. It reveals past, present, and future influences related to simple questions and is often recommended for beginner practitioners.

Here is how to cast it:

- Pull 3 runes out of your bag one at a time, and put them onto the cloth. Make sure you place them side by side with their symbols facing you.
- The first rune indicates your issue in general, so make sure you take a good look at it.
- The second rune shows all the challenges you face as a result of the issue.
- The last rune highlights potential steps you can take to overcome the challenges.

The 5-Rune Layout

Once you get the hang of the 3-rune spread, you can try your hand at the 5-rune layout. The 2 additional runes will help you to explore your issue in detail so you can better understand how your future will be influenced by your past and present.

Here is how to do the 5-rune spread:

- Lay out your runes in the shape of a cross. The bottom rune will represent the fundamental influences over the answers you seek.
- The rune on the far left conveys the problems that lead to the questions.
- The rune on the far right represents the answers to your questions.
- The rune on the top indicates positive influences over the question and answers.

- The last rune, the one in the middle, indicates any possible future influences over the answer.

The 7-Rune Layout

The 7-rune layout reveals past, present, and future influences related to your questions, along with other possible issues you weren't aware of - some of which you may want to explore further.

Here is how to use the 7-rune spread:

- With the runes in your hand, formulate a question (or more).
- Lay out your runes in a V shape and start interpreting the answers and the possible influences over them.
- The first rune in the top left position indicates influences from the past.
- The second rune under it represents the current influences related to the answers.
- The one that follows below shows how future actions may influence the outcome and the truthfulness of the answers.
- The central rune at the bottom of the V indicates possible paths you can take to reach the desired outcome.
- The first rune on the right side above the center highlights any emotions that may influence the questions.
- The rune above it indicates any problems that lead to the question which may influence the outcome.
- Finally, the rune on the top right represents the possible future outcomes of the situation or question you want to learn about.

The 9-Rune Layout

9 is considered a mystical number in Norse mythology, and using them in a rune layout can improve your divination practice. It's also incredibly easy to use, even though it requires 9 different symbols to interpret. Here is how to do it:

- Close your eyes, and scatter 9 runes on a cloth.
- Open your eyes and look at how they landed while paying attention to two factors.

- Are the runes turned over or facing upward? Runes that land on the right side uphold the answer to your questions, while the ones facing down indicate issues related to the questions you aren't aware of yet.
- You should also look at whether the runes have landed closer to the center of the cloth or further away. The former shows the crucial matters you should be concerned about in the future, whereas the latter group pertains to less significant matters.

The 24-Rune Layout

A 24-rune layout is recommended for the beginning of a cycle to reveal what the year may bring you. Apart from the Roman calendar, New Year's Day, the beginning of one's birth year, and the winter solstice also count as the beginning of a new cycle. It's an advanced method as it uses all the 24 runes of the Elder Futhark.

Here is how to do the 24-runic layout spread:

- After formulating your questions, lay out your spread in a 3x8 grid. You will read and interpret each row from right to left.
- The first rune of the first row represents the ways you can obtain financial gain and prosperity.
- The second rune shows the ways you can improve your physical health and strength.
- The third rune shows how you can defend yourself and win over the competition.
- The fourth rune indicates how you can gain wisdom and inspiration for making changes.
- The fifth rune shows you the direction your life path will take during the year.
- The sixth rune reveals all the wisdom you may learn in the upcoming year.
- The seventh rune shows all the skills you can master and hone and the gifts you'll be given.
- The eight runes of the first row represent all the ways you can achieve balance and happiness.

- The first rune of the second row represents the future changes you can expect in your life.
- The second rune indicates what you need to do to achieve your dreams and obtain your goals.
- The third rune represents any obstacles life may throw in your way on your journey.
- The fourth rune highlights your achievements and successes throughout the year.
- The fifth rune indicates any challenges you'll need to conquer and the choices you'll need to make.
- The sixth rune represents all your inner strength and skills that'll manifest.
- The seventh rune represents the most critical situation you'll face during the year.
- The eighth rune will act as a guide for your energy on your journey.
- The first rune of the third row represents any business and legal matters you're a part of.
- The second rune shows how you'll achieve personal growth.
- The third rune indicates all the relationships you'll make and juggle in the upcoming year.
- The fourth rune represents your expected social status.
- The fifth rune shows you how your emotional status may change.
- The sixth rune highlights any romantic situation you'll be part of.
- The seventh rune shows you the ways you will obtain harmony in your life.
- The eighth rune represents all the assets you'll gain throughout the year.

How to Read Each Rune

Once you have your runes spread in front of you, you'll be able to interpret their meanings. The table below shows a quick recap of the primary meaning of each runic symbol.

Freyr's Aett		Heimdall's Aett		Tyr's Aett	
Fehu ᚠ	Cattle/ Wealth	Hagalaz ᚺ	Hail	Tiwaz ᛏ	Victory
Uruz ᚢ	Ox	Nautiz ᚾ	Needs	Berkana ᛒ	Birch
Thurisaz ᚦ	Giant/ Thorn	Isa ᛁ	Ice	Ehwaz ᛖ	Horse
Ansuz ᚨ	Message	Jera ᛃ	Harvest	Mannaz ᛗ	Man
Raido ᚱ	Journey	Eihwaz ᛇ	Yew	Laguz ᛚ	Lake
Kenaz ᚲ	Torch	Pertrho ᛈ	Destiny	Ingwaz ᛝ	Fertility
Gebo ᚷ	Gift	Algiz ᛉ	Elk	Dagaz ᛞ	Dawn
Wunjo ᚹ	Joy	Sowilo ᛊ	Sun	Othila ᛟ	Heritage

However, as you've learned from the previous chapters, each rune of the Elder Futhark has several symbolic associations. For example, Ehwaz means horse, but it's also believed to mean luck or wheel. To get the answers you seek, it's crucial to not only focus on the primary meanings. Instead, you should think about each rune meaning how they relate to your questions. If we follow the example of Ehwaz, you should consider whether your question was about luck, possible travel, sports involving wheels, or horses in general. Think about your situation as well - the questions you ask may not convey what you really want to achieve because you aren't aware of it consciously. For example, if you are down on your luck and Ehwaz comes up in the primary answer position, you should look at the other runes for answers on how you may change your luck. Don't disregard your gut feelings because these are often the key to unlocking the unconscious answers your conscious mind can't process. For example, if you see Ehwaz and your immediate thought is that you are about to get a promotion at your job, there is a high chance that you'll be right.

Chapter 8: More Ways to Work with Runes

While most of the time, Norse runes are used for divinatory practices, they can also be a powerful addition to your meditation and magic rituals. You can select one or more runes associated with your intention for the rite and incorporate them into your practice. Not only that, but you can also wear them every day as a talisman to remind you of the intention you've set when charging the rune. This chapter covers several uses for runes - from meditation to making love talismans to Runic Reiki. Most of these options require you to use runic magic alongside other tools, which you are free to choose depending on what you feel you need to manifest your intention.

Using Runes in Rituals

Using runes in rituals requires regular practice because it increases focus and improves intuitive skills. The more you practice, the more vividly you can visualize runes, which, in turn, will significantly expand your ability to manifest your intent. The number of ways you can use runes in rituals is virtually limitless, as they can be incorporated into every type of ceremony. Here are a few simple ones to help you get started.

Rune Connection Empowering Exercise

Even if you've found the rune you feel drawn to and charged it with your energy, you may still want to strengthen your bond with it. Beginners can especially take advantage of this simple exercise. Here is how to perform this ritual:

- Cut out a 3x5 inch piece of paper and draw the rune you've chosen on it with a red marker.
- Sit in a comfortable position in front of your altar or table and place the paper in front of you.
- Take a couple of deep breaths while you focus on forming the rune in your mind.
- Repeat the name of the rune three times in your mind, or if you feel that it improves your concentration, you can also chant it out loud.
- Pause after the third time to see what the rune is telling you, then repeat its name three more times.
- Continue this for several minutes until you form a solid mental image of the shape of the rune - and its connection to the sensations running through your body and mind.
- The overall exercise should last no more than 10 minutes, but if you feel that you need more time to perfect your posture, breathing and focus, feel free to do it for as long as you want.

Ritual for Improving Your Focus

If you still have trouble maintaining your concentration, this exercise can help you improve this skill so you can manifest your intention. It's very similar to the previous one, except it focuses more on regulating breath patterns. Here is how to do it:

- Repeat the first step from the previous exercise up until you are getting ready to recite the name of the symbol.
- Here, you want to do this out loud while maintaining a specific breathing pattern. This involves inhaling for 10 seconds, holding your breath for 2 seconds, and releasing it

along with the name of the symbol. Hold your breath once again for 2 seconds.

- Now, try shifting your position to see if it improves your concentration. For example, try standing up or laying down if you are sitting. If you were standing, sit down with your shoulders relaxed.
- Once you've found the position that works best for you, focus on the paper in front of you for a couple of minutes.
- Close your eyes and visualize the symbol in front of you. Try creating as vivid an image of it as possible.
- Once you can maintain the image in front of you for 10 minutes, you've successfully mastered this exercise.

Protection Ritual

Runic protection rituals were also popular among the ancient Norse. Apart from deterring negative influences from one's life, a protection ritual can also be performed to banish forces that may interfere with the work of the practitioner. Here is a protection rite you can practice every day and use in conjunction with any other ritual:

- Stand in a comfortable position and set a relaxing breathing rhythm. You can either follow the pattern described in the previous exercise or create your own.
- With your eyes closed or open, visualize either the Hagalaz or Eihwaz runes in red while chanting the sound out loud three times.
- Slowly turn in a circle while maintaining the image of the rune and repeating its name, and take on a steady and deep breathing rhythm.
- Once you can perform this exercise without breaks in your concentration, you will be able to undertake any other rune work with confidence.

Opening Ritual

In ancient times, powerful work with runic magic often required the practitioner to perform an invocatory ritual before the actual act. This helped prepare the practitioner's mind, body, and space for the process so they could manifest their intention more effectively. It typically also addresses a Norse deity who will be asked for assistance during the main ritual. If you wish to incorporate this ritual into your practice, you can do it by following this guide:

- Stand in the middle of a room or sacred space you've chosen to perform your ritual in, facing east or north.
- Holding the runes you'll be working with through the main ritual, recite the following:

  "Fare now mighty (the name of the Norse deity whom you are working with) from your heavenly home.

  Swiftly ride with all your might to help us give and gain.

  Holy runes we now use to draw the powers,

  the steady stream they flow with is now ours."

- Now walk to the most eastern or northern part of your space and, with your hand, trace a circle following the sun, left to right, while chanting:

  "These mighty runes are now drawn around us,

  unwanted forces; now stay away!"

- When you've completed the circle, return to the center of the space, facing the same direction as you did before. After that chant:

  "The worrisome forces are now on their way towards the east,

  hallowed be your name, oh mighty (name of Norse deity)."

- Once this invocatory ritual is completed, you can perform the primary rite.

Closing Ritual

When a magical act began with an opening ritual, the ancient Norse were also compelled to use a closing rite. This is used for the assimilation of messages received during the ritual and as an expression of gratitude for the help of the deities. This further fortifies the intent of the ritual. Here is how you can perform a successful closing ritual:

- Stand facing east or north while intoning:

  "Now the holy work is done with the help of (Norse deity).

  We hail to them because we know they granted us their help."
- Now, it's time for you to extinguish any candles or fire that's traditionally used during rituals.
- Hold or trace the Kenaz symbol and say the following:
- *"With the help of fire that's now ceased to glow, may forever be kindled with the mighty (Norse deity)."*
- If you've performed an empowering magic act, this may require you to internalize your newfound energy. So, the next step is to draw it in with the help of the Fehu rune.
- You can either hold this in your hand or draw its likeness in the air with your hand and take deep breaths.
- Draw your arms in, touching your solar plexus with your fingertips.
- Repeat this in all four cardinal directions, each time visualizing the energy being drawn into your center.
- With a last exhale of the exercise, let go of any images you've focused on during the rite and step away from the sacred space.

Runic Meditation

While a form of runic meditation has been covered in a previous chapter, this one brings a general type of meditation you can tailor to your preferences and magical needs.

Runic meditation can help you align your energy.

https://unsplash.com/photos/FjYwhowyp6k

Whichever magic act you decide to perform, this mediation can help you prepare for it by ensuring your energy is aligned with your needs. Here is how to do a runic meditation exercise:

- Find a quiet place where you won't be disturbed and are able to feel comfortable enough, and make this your dedicated meditation area.
- Using the symbols you feel drawn to at present, create a ring rune on a larger sheet of paper and place it in front of you so it'll be at eye level when meditating.
- Assume a comfortable position and take a few deep breaths.
- When you are relaxed enough, look at a rune ring in front of you.
- Now, you can step onto a secondary level of consciousness by placing the runes in the center of your focus.
- Concentrate on what the rune ring represents for you and how you plan to use it.
- Now, slowly close your eyes and continue visualizing the form of each rune as they appear on the paper.
- Contemplate their likeness in your mind's eye and listen to your intuition.
- If you are a beginner, you may have trouble focusing on the images with your eyes closed. If so, feel free to open your eyes and look at the symbols before closing them again.
- Having mastered the focus, you move on to a more complex analysis of the runes.
- In the beginning, you can maintain your focus on each rune for 10-15 seconds in an attempt to decipher them. After some practice, you'll be able to do this within 5 seconds per rune.
- After this, you should take a deep, cleansing breath and lapse into inner silence.
- During this, the runes you've visualized are being paired up with a resounding intent and purpose.

- You may continue the meditation as long as you feel a link with the runic force. In this meditative state, you may be led along numerous paths. Some will be associated with the rune itself, while others will reveal relationships between the runes. Either way, the possibilities for using runes meditation are infinite.
- Once you feel the link to the rune dissipating, you can end the meditation by taking a deep breath. If you wish, you can also repeat a closing statement similar to the following:

  "Now my work is done, and I am ready to go on."

- Open your eyes and break the ritual by stepping away from the meditation area.

Runic Talismans

Runes don't have to be limited to meditative or ritual uses. You can also benefit from their energy by wearing them as a talisman. With the symbol associated with what you want to achieve close to you, focusing on manifesting your intention in real life will be much easier.

Choose a rune that you really feel a connection with, as these will be in alignment with your intuition. Runic talismans are generally made from stone, wood, bone, or metal, although parchment paper was also used occasionally. Any one of these will work if you keep it on your desk or carry it around as a pendant.

The objects on which the runes are carved may also serve some utilitarian functions, such as pens, buckles, automobiles, and more. The following simple runic talismans and inscription formulas can be of help.

Encouraging or Binding Love

One of the most popular ways to use runes as talismans is to encourage love and affection to develop a relationship or strengthen the bond within an existing one. Remember that you can't create affection where there isn't any, and the runes should be used for good intentions. Apart from the ethical implications, love magic seems to work more effectively when it's used to enhance existing feelings. Here is how to create a talisman for love rituals:

- Create the runes by carving the following symbols into a piece of wood or stone:
- ᚷᚨᚾᛏᛖᚦ
- Carve the name of the two people between whom you want to enhance the affection on the other side of the talisman.
- Whether you are making the talisman to enhance your love life or someone else's, make two sets so the spell can work on both sides.
- After etching the names and symbols into the runes, you should charge the runes with your intention. Do this by focusing on the two people you want to bring together - as well as on the runic forces that'll bind the love.
- The two people the rune is meant for should wear the talisman close to their bodies to encourage affection from the other person. An alternate form of this ritual is etching the symbols into a pre-made piece of wooden or stone jewelry, which makes it easier to wear.
- The two parties can also place the talisman under each other's bed or over a threshold the other person regularly crosses.

Following a centuries-old tradition, practitioners of Norse magic often gift love charms to each other as part of their wedding ceremony. A modern take on this is for couples to express the strength of their bond by making elaborate invitations for wedding ceremonies, handfasting rituals, and any celebration they hold together.

Talisman for Wisdom

Talismans can also be used to gather wisdom. You will need a talisman, tools for making it, and a cup of wine or grape juice.

- If you are making the talisman by painting a rune onto it, make sure you use natural products instead of artificial coloring.
- If you are carving the runes, don't etch them too deeply into the surface either.

- While you can use several types of runes for a wisdom talisman, Mannaz works best to unlock new information for the conscious mind.
- Collect the shavings into a container and mix them with honey or mead. Repeat the following:

  "As I mix these runes, the sweet source of wisdom,

  They will blend together in a powerful bond."

  Take the cup into your hands and drink its content.
- Your energy is now absorbing inspiration and wisdom.
- You can wear the talisman or give it to someone who can benefit from the additional knowledge. The person wearing it will attract a wealth of information they can use to improve their lives.

Runic Healing and Reiki

Norse runes can also be used for healing, whether in Pagan-based or any other type of healing practice. An interesting use of runes for healing is combining them with the traditional Reiki symbols. This method is based on the Runic Reiki system, where both Norse and Reiki symbols are activated similarly, and the practitioner applies visualization to put them to use. What makes Runic Reiki so valuable is that it makes it easier to practice healing as it requires no hand placement as the traditional techniques do. This also makes Runic Reiki perfect for distance healing. Here is how to use this method:

- Start by visualizing the healing symbol to help diminish the effect of the distance between you and the recipient.
- Hold the Shai Nal Reiki symbol in your hands, as this will help you increase your power.
- Visualize tracing a line around the recipient's body with the Shai Nal symbol. It should start above their head and finish at their second chakra.
- Active Shail Nal by reciting its name three times in a row in your head.
- Within the lines of this symbol, you'll visualize a Norse rune associated with the body part you are trying to heal.

- For example, if you want to alleviate an emotional trauma, you will use Laguz. Whereas if you want to heal a physical injury or ailment, you will need to use Ehwaz. You can also use Mannaz to clear your mind and Uruz and Fehu to improve someone's health.
- Now, you should change your focus with the help of the Han-so symbol.
- Recite some position affirmations, such as:

  "You feel healthy and radiant."

  "You are not in pain."
- Statements that convey positive messages are easier for your subconscious to process, as it finds it harder to negative statements.
- Maintain the image of Shai Nal over the recipient and try to see them being surrounded by pink or red light.
- Use the Reloxone Reiki symbols to form a connection with a specific power source, like a Norse deity or any other guide you may use.
- When you have finished, seal your healing by visually combining the distance healing symbol with Algiz (for another layer of protection) or Sowilo (to thank your guide for allowing you to heal).

Chapter 9: Norse Magic in the Modern World

In modern times, Norse traditions are not directly related to the Vikings' beliefs. Due to the limited number of written sources on the subject, we have more of an interpretation of this old religion. Therefore, modern-day practitioners do what they feel is right for them.

Unlike most other religions, the Norse faith doesn't have one book with all the answers. Most followers will have a unique and individual way of doing things. The Poetic Edda, of course, is a wonderful resource that shows the original tales of the gods and their practices with runes and divination. But it's not going to give you everything you need to familiarize yourself with this religion.

For you to be able to develop your own method of practicing Norse magic, it is necessary to examine how modern-day practitioners use Norse magic and its traditions. The first thing you need to do is understand how Norse magic made its way into modern-day faith and how it has influenced the way we live. After that, you can decide if you want to practice individually or within a community, as there are just as many methods of community practice as there are independent ones. Following that, we will discuss a few ways in which you can incorporate Norse magic into your daily life and make it part of your everyday routine.

Ásatrú (Ásatrúarfélagið)

The Old Norse paganism Ásatrú, the religion of the original Viking settlers, is going through a renaissance of sorts. Spiritual paths rooted in the Norse ancestors' practices and beliefs are common in modern society. Some Norse Pagans refer to themselves as Heathens, but many refer to themselves as Asatru.

Asatru was the name created by Nordic Neo-pagans during the Middle Ages. This term was coined in the 19th century to describe the reconstruction of the religious traditions of Scandinavia from before Christianity was introduced. In this time period, the 19th century, Asatru roughly translated as "to be true to the Aesir," one of the Norse God tribes (Odin, Höðr, Baldr, Frigg, Thor, Freyr, and Freyja). Aesir, the main group of the Norse Gods, became the focus of the Asatru religion. The term refers to a set of religions and spiritualities that originates from Northern European spiritual beliefs.

Asatru concept then refers to being faithful to the Norse gods while also recognizing pagan traditions from the pre-Christian Scandinavian era, leading to the creation of new branches of this faith.

Modern-Day Ásatrú

Sveinbjorn Beinteinsson played an essential role in establishing Asatru's recognition by the Icelandic government in 1972 during the late 1960s and early 1970s. At this point, several Asatru organizations began to appear throughout Europe and America. Many people worldwide follow Asatru, primarily in organizations in the United States and Europe, and it is even recognized as an official religion in certain European countries.

There is a great emphasis on Norse myths in Asatru, even though they are not considered historical facts. Instead, they are seen as a guide to achieving greatness, enjoying the world, and utilizing everything around us to our advantage. We humans have an intimate relationship with the gods since they are often seen as part of nature. However, we only turn to the gods for help when all human efforts, resources, and every single other option have been exhausted. Worshiping the Norse gods calls for a gift. As a result, sacrifices are often made in the form of ceremonies in which food, drink, and personal items are shared. This is done to maintain a strong bond between the gods and us.

According to the adherents of the Asatru tradition, objects are considered to be an important part of the connection between human beings and the gods. There is a possibility that objects can be infused with power by the gods. It is believed that all things within the universe are connected to each other by a flow of energy. As an example, we may create a rune charm or divination set. In a sense, we are binding our essence to it. By giving it shape, we give it a part of ourselves and, as an offering, we can give this to the gods. In exchange, the gods provide us with power and enthusiasm that will help us live our lives on our own. The gods are manifestations of spiritual reality, which, in turn, affects us.

Followers of Asatru do not pray to the Gods. Instead of relying on formal rites, they meditate and seek their blessings through informal rituals. This aspect of honor is in itself a form of prayer to live a good and moral life and expresses the love of freedom because it is non-authoritarian and decentralized. Asatru has no all-powerful spiritual leader dictating truth to the world. There is no direct connection between a guru or priest and the Gods; instead, it is believed that the gods are a part of you.

Ásatrú as an Organization

The religion does, however, have some hierarchies based on specific organizations. An Asatru organization is known as a Kindred. A Kindred's priests are known as Gothar, which is a plural form of Gothi or Gythia. A Gothar is the Asatru community's collective priesthood, and Folk is its congregation. Like many pagan religions, this one emphasizes community as an essential aspect of its practice. Each member of the community has an important role to play in forming a unified force that benefits the whole. This way, the community is protected, fertile, prosperous, and well-off.

The Gothar are the collective priesthood of the Asatru Community. It translates to those who speak the godly tongue. A member of the Gothar is a highly visible member of the greater Asatru Community. People who wish to become Gothar must possess three things: Odin's wisdom, Thor's strength, and Freyja's love. Asatru worships these three primary deities. The three aspects are often expressed through sacred texts, belonging to a kindred and caring for the folk. In addition to guiding the folk with wisdom, being strong for the community and working for the benefit of the community requires a certain amount of love, friendship, and compassion. They are generally expected to conduct themselves in a way that sets an excellent example for others to follow. They play an essential role in the legacy and history of those who practice Asatru. The Althing, a high council of Asatru, sets the bylaws that the Folk must adhere to. Speakers of the Althing, the prominent voice of the council, are chosen by their kindred.

Asatru is a religion that shapes itself to modern needs and, as such, many Asatru organizations may do things differently, but the canons of this religion are the aforementioned basics.

Different Ásatrú Organizations

There is a wondrous variety of modern-day Asatru spiritualities based on pagan traditions. Asatru is the most famous neo-pagan branch, and there are differences from organization to organization. For example, one will focus solely on the Aesir, that is, Odin, Höðr, Baldr, Frigg, Thor, Freyr, and Freyja; sky gods, war gods, law, justice, poetry, and wisdom. Others are more focused on social realities and the need to maintain order with emphasis on fertility, prosperity, plenty, and magic.

In other words, Asatru is a neo-pagan polytheistic reconstruction based on certain religious and historical aspects of pre-Christian Scandinavia, a revival of the pre-Christian indigenous religion of the Norse people.

The followers of this faith, however, acknowledge that other people have their own gods as well as interacting with the Norse gods. It is important to note that Asatru followers do not believe that their gods represent the only true gods. No hierarchical structures, dogmas, or sacred books are at the center of the religion, which is a reconstruction of a religious tradition. Due to this, religious practices may differ in interpretation based on their environment.

Odinism

Odinism is another form of Norse theology organization. It's named after the god Odin. Reconstructed in modern times as a religion concerned with Germanic paganism, runes, mythology, and folklore. The first mention of Odinism dates back to the 1820s. In 1840, the term was used by Thomas Carlyle, a Scottish essayist, historian, and philosopher. Those who practice Odinism are associated with pagans and even white supremacists. Those who practice under Odin are often seen wearing a pendant with Thor's hammer around their necks.

Across Europe and parts of America, Odinism would continue to be practiced and altered ever since its inception. Today, there is very little research about Odinism because it has been erased and changed throughout history. Especially as Christianity made its way through the world. When Christianity came through, they heavily shunned paganism of any kind, including Odinism.

In the mid-1970s, the Committee for the Restoration of the Odinic Rite or Odinist Committee was founded in Britain. It represents a modern-day revival of Norse magical practices under the term Odinism. In 1980, the organization changed its name to The Odinic Rite following the increased interest in restoring the Odinic faith.

Modern Odinism beliefs are polytheistic, meaning they believe in more than one deity. The Viking era represents just a tiny portion of the evolution and history of the Odinic Rite. They disdain terms like Viking religion or Asatru.

According to the Odinic Rite, members should live according to the Nine Noble Virtues, based on writing found in the Poetic Edda like The Sigrdrífomál and The Hávamál:

- Self-reliance
- Perseverance
- Discipline
- Honor
- Courage
- Industriousness
- Hospitality
- Fidelity
- Truth

Modern Day Practice of Norse Magic

There is a general consensus that magic can be divided into good magic and evil magic. As common as this is among general populations, it is also prevalent in theories. The pre-Christian Germanic peoples, however, had fundamentally different ideas about magic and used it in various ways. As a result, modern magic involves tuning oneself in to nature and discerning fate to accomplish one's goals.

Going It Alone

The fact that there is no one way to practice is compelling to many followers. You have to discover everything for yourself. But it is through this self-discovery and research that you're going to learn and become a better version of yourself. As you go along this path, you may discover that there is a lot of alone time involved. Unlike other organizations, there is a lack of community-based learning and practice involved. Solitary worship of the gods and divination practice take place alone because it's a nature-based religion, one that involves personal growth and self-exploration. It is also an exploration of a relationship with the gods, so you will spend a lot of time with candles, fires, books, and runes. Learning more about the gods and the faith ties heavily into practice and research.

Community

Despite this solitary aspect of Modern day Norse practice, a knowledgeable community exists. Once you know how to find your fellow practitioners, you can start learning more and more. Meeting others that have had unique experiences and talking and learning from them is possible. Social media is a great way to connect with others who share your beliefs and interests. Other practitioners meet up to attend gatherings, and the community aspect of their respective religions can inspire you to continue on your path of divination, magic, and faith.

Gatherings

The old Nordic religion is still practiced openly - just like it was during the Viking age. Some practitioners praise and make offerings, toasts are drunk, and feasts are eaten to honor them. While some individuals will wish for prosperity and health by toasting the fertility gods Frej and Njörd, others can invoke Odin for wisdom or praise Thor for strength when facing a challenge. Some Nordic believers will gather in groups and go to specific sites to worship the gods and their magic. They will make offerings at pre-Christian cult sites to feel the power of their ancestors. Among the possible locations are Bronze

Age burial mounds or Viking Age ship settings. There is usually a ceremonial circle formed between the participants. Within the circle, this creates a "holy space" that connects to the gods' world. The circle is then ceremonially closed again after the participants have paid their respects to their gods. A total of four offerings are brought to the altar each year during the summer, solstice, winter solstice, autumn solstice, and spring equinox.

These group meetings are usually made up of individual practitioners. But there are organizations like Odinism and Asatru that hold weekly services.

Daily Practices to Incorporate into Your Life

In Norse-related activities, each individual worships the gods and nature in their own way. Whichever method works best for them is correct.

Amulets and Charms

Amulets have been used for thousands of years.
https://unsplash.com/photos/rsjwsaTLGgE

For thousands of years, people have worn specific Norse-related jewelry as a way to signify their faith. And to this day, there are thousands of people around the world who do the same thing. Whether in the form of Mjölnir (Thor's hammer) or rune charms, it's a powerful method to help reflect on what these things symbolize; Thor's guidance for strength but also the protection of the gods and your honor to them.

Nature

Take 10 or 15 minutes to sit outside every day. No matter what the weather, observe the world around you and really think about your faith. Because nature is such an essential aspect of this faith, finding a place you can escape to for just a few minutes every day will make a massive difference in how you connect with it. You need nature to separate you from the outside world. Whether it's a single tree, a bush, a patch of grass, or even a potted plant in your home, find somewhere that you can just disappear and reconnect to nature, even for a few minutes.

Don't Expect Results Straight Away

By adhering to the Norse traditions' beliefs, you will have these big moments of realization and awareness. They may not happen every day or every week. They may not even happen every month. For the most part, we live our lives as we normally do, but it is still possible to bring a little bit more faith and rhythm into them with each little step we make toward understanding these complex traditions. So, it's important not to expect too much too soon. The big moments will come when they're meant to. The gods will show you the signs when you're meant to see them. And in the meantime, there is nothing wrong with enjoying a little bit of peace to sit back and enjoy nature and take note of the small signs in everyday life.

Indoor Altar

Another great way to incorporate the Norse traditions into your life is by creating an indoor altar. It can be in any style or size you want. Some people will have a Thor figure, along with some herbs, candles, and incense. While others will fill their table with their runes, charms, and crystals. This allows practitioners to feel connected to the gods while away from home. It can create tremendous strength and determination throughout the day to know they are there when you get home. You could also build an outdoor altar to represent your attachment to the natural world. Maintaining your altar and keeping it clean and organized while decorating it in any way you like is a great way to connect with your faith and the magical possibilities it can provide.

A shrine can just as easily be included in an offering to the gods. Spending time in front of your shrine or altar for the gods, ancestors, or spirits and meditating can help you feel connected to it.

Our previous discussion has emphasized the importance of the small details in your Norse venture. It is not possible for us to hunt a wild boar for sacrifice to Odin like the Vikings or our pagan ancestors. So, making these small offerings is an honorable way to pay homage to the history of Norse tradition, even if we cannot do it on a large scale.

There are various ways you can stay connected and get an extra moment to reflect on your journey. If you have anything you do that you believe might be helpful to others, or if you just want to share your story or share your daily rituals as a Norse Pagan, you can share them with the world. Creating a platform to tell your tale, whether it is on social media, a website, or in a book, can be great ways to learn from your experiences and inspire others along the way. Being able to stay connected outside of those important moments of life is one of the most challenging disciplines of this faith.

Having read this chapter on the traditions of Norse magic and its uses in modern society, you have taken one of the most important steps along your magical journey. There is no doubt that this will help you expand your spiritual horizons, and you will have a better understanding of other spiritual realities, which, in turn, will help you to take that step forward, go over the fence, and gradually leap into the possibilities of Norse magic.

Bonus: List of Runes and Their Symbolism

In this section, you will find a quick reference guide to all of the Elder Futhark runes. Listed are the names of the runes, the Aetts they belong to, and their corresponding places within each Aett. You can refer back to this page whenever you need a refresher on the pronunciation of rune names or the meaning of their magical symbolism.

Aettir (plural form of aett) is the term used to divide the Elder Futhark runes into three equal parts. The division enables students to study in a structured manner. Before moving on to the next aett, many people like to understand the previous one better. The themes of each Aett are different, but there are also some commonalities. While each aett is singularly unique on its own, they each also represent luminosity in one way or another. All three Aett have a rune that represents wealth in some way and at least one that represents danger.

The First Aett: Freya's Aett

The first Aett belongs to Freya, the Norse goddess of beauty, fertility, and love. This collection of runes is about enjoyment, love, emotions, happiness, and physical presence. It also refers to creation, growth, and beginnings.

Freya's Aett represents the nurturer, the mother, the farmer, and the merchant. It is also the Aettir of the first degree as it represents the cycle of life.

In Freyr's Aett, the runes represent what it takes to live a fulfilling life, to experience and interact with other humans, and to experience the divine.

FEHU

Letter Value: F

English Pronunciation: "FAY-hoo"

Translation: Cattle, prosperity, property, hope, happiness, abundance, wealth, and financial gain.

Magical Symbolism: Achieve goals, luck, new beginnings, abundance, success, luck.

In Practice: Focus its energies where you wish to experience the most success in your life, as it represents abundance, achievement, and prosperity.

URUZ

Letter Value: U

English Pronunciation: "OO-rooz"

Translation: Wild ox, unexpected change, life force, indomitability, strength, power, and good mental and physical health.

Magical Symbolism: Understanding, strength, speed, energy, courage, dedication, vitality.

In Practice: Uruz helps to shape the world around you. It can guide you both physically and mentally and can refer to many aspects of change - it could mean that you will have more strength or that you are going to be challenged in your strength. Uruz also deals with your past strength - your health and actions coming back to haunt you.

THURISAZ

Letter Value: TH

English Pronunciation: "THUR-ee-sazh"

Translation: Giant, god of Thunder, lightning, thorn, caution, defensive force, and disruption.

Magical Symbolism: Focus on getting rid of the negative, regeneration, concentration, and self-discipline.

In Practice: Thurisaz is both sides of the same coin - it can be about protection, but the same force that protects can also destroy. The name comes from "Thor," the god of lightning, and we know from legend that he can destroy as much as he can create.

ANSUZ

Letter Value: A

English Pronunciation: "AHN-sooz"

Translation: The All Father, Odin, and the other gods are represented by "A." It means wisdom, life, communing, mouth, listening, and prophecy.

Magical Symbolism: Leadership, communication, wisdom, signals, health.

In Practice: Ansuz is linked to Odin and the ancestral gods. It represents wise communication and well-intended listening- to yourself and others.

RAIDHO

Letter Value: R

English Pronunciation: "Rah-EED-ho"

Translation: Travel & change, rest & rhythm, journeying, wagon, momentum, the big picture.

Magical Symbolism: Bring about change, protection for travelers, rhythm, facilitate change, and reconnect.

In Practice: Raidho is the contemplation of achieving something and the discipline to follow through with it. This rune is the power to move forward toward our desired destinations.

KENAZ

Letter Value: K/C

English Pronunciation: "KEN-nahz"

Translation: Fire, energy, torch or beacon, light, passion, transform, and creation.

Magical Symbolism: Light, motivation, regeneration, inspiration, regeneration.

In Practice: As a torch, Kenaz illuminates the way through the darkness. Kenaz is the controlled energy or burning flame that can create and transform. When you look inside, you can find Kenaz - your burning passion. When you focus on your burning passion, you can keep out negative influences.

GEBO

Letter Value: G

English Pronunciation: "GHEH-boh"

Translation: Togetherness, gifting, generous, exchange, gratitude, giving & receiving, sacrifice (self), forgiving, and offering.

Magical Symbolism: Balance, luck, fertility, successful partnering, giving.

In Practice: The giving or receiving of a gift is represented by Gebo. We should receive a gift as well as we give one, and there should be no expectations about what we are about to receive or the other person's role in the process.

WUNJO

Letter Value: W

English Pronunciation: "WOON-yo"

Translation: Harmony, Fullness, joy, wellbeing, alignment, contentment, ecstasy, and balance.

Magical Symbolism: Happiness, harmony, joy, prosperity, success, motivation.

In Practice: Wunjo represents fulfilling goals. Whenever we are in harmony with our goals and working together, we will prosper and grow.

The Second Aett: Hagal's Aett

The Second Aett, Hagal, represents the forces that surround us. In most cases, these are not governed by intelligence - but by the forces of nature.

Hagal is a warrior. He shows unending courage and tenacity despite overwhelming odds. The key components of this Aett are money, accomplishments, power, victories, and success. A force outside our control is present in Hagal.

Neutrality is its defining characteristic. It is the runes of Hagal's Aett which speak to the unexpected occurrences in life, such as disruptions, changes, stalled progress, and unforeseen good fortune. Nothing lasts forever, so they help us get through the more challenging parts of our lives.

HAGALAZ

Letter Value: H

English Pronunciation: "HA-ga-lahz"

Translation: Hail, destruction, sudden difficulties, violent change of nature, and delay.

Magical Symbolism: Destructive, dangerous weather, breaking destructive patterns, the wrath of nature, uncontrolled forces.

In Practice: Hagalaz is about being patient and witting for what is coming your way. There might be obstacles, challenges, and delays, and you must accept this delay and disruption, content that it is part of your change and journey.

NAUTHIZ

Letter Value: N

English Pronunciation: "NOWD-heez"

Translation: Need, distress, desire for triumph, stagnation, and change manifestation.

Magical Symbolism: Survival, frustration, endurance, obstacles, determination.

In Practice: Naudhiz is a manifestation of distress, struggle, and need, but it is also a manifestation of overcoming those challenges.

ISA

Letter Value: I

English Pronunciation: "EEH-sah"

Translation: Cold, winter, ice, change, momentum, still, delay, waiting, new beginnings, and pauses.

Magical Symbolism: Reinforcement of other kinds of magic, ice, obstacles, blockages, freezing, reflection.

In Practice: Isa is the calm before the storm, the stillness that comes from the change in your life. When we feel we are stagnating, we are often not, and Isa is our old ways and habits that are ingrained into our minds. We need the stagnation to bring about the change.

JERA

Letter Value: J / Y

English Pronunciation: "YAR-ah"

Translation: Cycles, circles, time, movement, rewards, value, harvesting what has been sown, and the prize of our efforts.

Magical Symbolism: Fruition, eliminate stagnation, growth, harvest, create change.

In Practice: Night gives way to day. There are new cycles all around us, like dawn after the dark. A new cycle has begun, and with Jera, you are rewarded for your hard work put in.

EIHWAZ

Letter Value: E / I

English Pronunciation: "EYE-wahz"

Translation: The great yew tree, long life, wisdom, life & death, sacrifice, new beginnings, and moving on to the next stage.

Magical Symbolism: To ease a life transition, defense, transformation, protection, cause change.

In Practice: Eihwaz symbolizes the yew tree, which represents life and death. This death, however, is not always literal. Transitions can be signified by it. Closing the door to allow another to open. To move forward, you have to leave the past in the past.

PERTHRO

Letter Value: P

English Pronunciation: "PEHR-throw"

Translation: What is to come, mysteries, the hidden, secrets, the self, what is inside, fate, and casting.

Magical Symbolism: Knowledge of secrets, fertility, enhancing self and powers, control of uncertainty.

In Practice: Perthro represents Karma. Our current situation is a result of the actions we or someone else have taken in the past. It aids with contemplation.

ALGIZ

Letter Value: Z

English Pronunciation: "AHL-geez"

Translation: Luck, defense, good omens, elks, instinct & self-protection, safe haven, and the connection to what is more than you.

Magical Symbolism: Channeling energy, a shield, protection, ward against evil, guardian.

In Practice: Algiz is a force of protection. It can be a sign that one needs to seek refuge. Algiz is also an omen of luck, strengthening awareness and bringing guidance to those who need it.

SOWILO

Letter Value: S

English Pronunciation: "Soh-WEE-low"

Translation: Power, spirit, strength, health & vitality, enlightenment, energy, goodness, success, and your growth.

Magical Symbolism: Cosmic force, energy, healing, strength, cleansing, success.

In Practice: Sowilo cuts through the darkness and your own self-doubts - giving you the chance to grow and change, to expand to be the person you know you can be. You can find your purpose and look toward your ultimate goal.

The Third Aett: Tyr's Aett

This third set of runes addresses the internal forces we encounter as we travel the path outlined in the First Aett and deal with the external forces of the Second Aett.

As a symbol of victory and protection, Tyr symbolizes moral values, justice, spiritual attainment, understanding, atonement, establishing order, and all matters involving authority and politics. It focuses on intellectual development, understanding, and spiritual growth.

There are direct connections between the runes of Tyr's Aett and ancient deities, natural forces, and humanity itself, illustrating aspects of the dance between visible and invisible realms.

TIWAZ

Letter Value: T

English Pronunciation: "TEE-wahz"

Translation: The God Tyr, victory, bravery, courage, need for justice, honor, and sacrifice for the greater good.

Magical Symbolism: Victory, protection, reinforced will, strength, healing a wound, analysis.

In Practice: Tiwaz is a symbol of facing opposition with courage and is a direct influence from the Norse god of war and bloodshed, Tyr. Tiwaz means strength and fearlessness.

BERKANA

Letter Value: B

English Pronunciation: "BEHR-kah-nah"

Translation: New beginnings & rebirth, a change, new phases in life, relationships, projects, the birch tree, and the cycles of life.

Magical Symbolism: Starting again, encouragement, desire, healing, regeneration, liberation.

In Practice: Symbolizing life's transitions, Berkano represents growth and a new beginning. Berkano reminds us that every ending brings a fresh beginning, and every phase brings its own challenges and celebrations.

EHWAZ

ᛖ

Letter Value: E

English Pronunciation: "EH-wahz"

Translation: Partnership & cooperation, horses, loyalty, moving forward, progress, and workmen together.

Magical Symbolism: Energy, power, trust, progress, communication, progress, change, transportation.

In Practice: Ehwaz represents a collaborative effort to incite change and progress. Trust and loyalty are essential for successful relationships between partners or between the conflicting parts of ourselves.

MANNAZ

Letter Value: M

English Pronunciation: "MAN-az"

Translation: Divine & human potential, wisdom, intelligence, reasoning, traditions & habits, self-development, balance, and reason.

Magical Symbolism: Order in life, intelligence, thought, ability, skill, create.

In Practice: Mannaz symbolizes intelligence, rationality, and tradition. The pursuit of a perfect balance in life is self-development. The Mannaz rune can help you increase rational thought and gain control over your emotions.

LAGUZ

ᛚ

Letter Value: L

English Pronunciation: "LAH-good"

Translation: Water, intuition, flow, cleansing, inward journey, personality depth.

Magical Symbolism: Stabilize emotions and turmoil, enhance psychic abilities, uncover the truth, and confront fears.

In Practice: All life comes from water, which is represented by Laguz. In the same way, water symbolizes our emotional journey and the flow of our lives. Through it, we can deal with difficult growth and transition through life's transitions.

INGWAZ

Letter Value: NG

English Pronunciation: "ING-wahz"

Translation: Sexuality, fertility, self-development, energy, potential, family, ancestors, and doing things at the right time.

Magical Symbolism: Strength, growth, health, balance, grounded, connect.

In Practice: Potential energy is represented by Ingwaz. A reminder that things cannot be rushed. The rune helps you to prepare for what is to come, so you have the energy ready to be transformed - aiding your patience and building your strength.

DAGAZ

Letter Value: D

English Pronunciation: "DAH-gahz"

Translation: Immediate change, the coming light, the illumination of the gods, self-betterment, inspiration, wisdom, the day.

Magical Symbolism: Clarity, positivity, awakening, awareness, transformation.

In Practice: A new era begins with Dagaz, which represents divine inspiration and the end of an era. By going with the flow and enjoying the beauty of life, you will find your muse all around you.

OTHALA

Letter Value: O

English Pronunciation: "Oh-THA-la"

Translation: Spirit, wisdom, intelligence, talent, welcoming, community, people, ancestors, physical buildings, and finding your roots.

Magical Symbolism: Influence over possessions, inheritance, experience, ancestry, heritage, and value.

In Practice: We have a legacy with Othala. We all have both the material and spiritual around us. OTHALA represents the spiritual and material assets we have attained. We must use Othala to better build and grow our lives.

Here's another book by Mari Silva that you might like

Your Free Gift
(only available for a limited time)

Thanks for getting this book! If you want to learn more about various spirituality topics, then join Mari Silva's community and get a free guided meditation MP3 for awakening your third eye. This guided meditation mp3 is designed to open and strengthen ones third eye so you can experience a higher state of consciousness. Simply visit the link below the image to get started.

https://spiritualityspot.com/meditation

References

Futhark Magic: A Study of Ancient Runes - SnitchSeeker.com. (n.d.). Snitchseeker.Com. https://www.snitchseeker.com/term-27-january-april-2011/futhark-magic-a-study-of-ancient-runes-78018/

Dan. (2012, November 14). *Runes.* Norse Mythology for Smart People. https://norse-mythology.org/runes/

Dan. (2013, June 29). *Runic Philosophy and Magic.* Norse Mythology for Smart People. https://norse-mythology.org/runes/runic-philosophy-and-magic/

Gol stave church. (2019, April 13). Stavechurch.com. https://www.stavechurch.com/gol-stave-church/?lang=en

Harper, B. (2018, October 15). *47 Harry Potter spells to memorize while you're waiting for your Hogwarts letter.* Fatherly. https://www.fatherly.com/entertainment/25-harry-potter-spells-charms-everyone-should-know

McKay, A. (2020, August 21). *Viking runes: The historic writing systems of northern Europe.* Life in Norway. https://www.lifeinnorway.net/viking-runes/

Page, R. I. (1998). *Runes and runic inscriptions: Collected essays on Anglo-Saxon and viking runes.* Boydell Press.

Runemarks: Using runes. (n.d.). Joanne-harris.co.uk. http://www.joanne-harris.co.uk/books/runemarks/runemarks-using-runes/

Runer og magi. (n.d.). Avaldsnes. https://avaldsnes.info/en/viking/lorem-ipsum/

S., J. (2021, April 27). *How to read rune stones.* Norse and Viking Mythology [Best Blog] - Vkngjewelry; vkngjewelry. https://blog.vkngjewelry.com/en/rune-divination-how-to-read-the-runes/

Sørensen, A. C., & Horte, R. M. J. (n.d.). *Runes.* Vikingeskibsmuseet i Roskilde. https://www.vikingeskibsmuseet.dk/en/professions/education/viking-age-people/runes

Thornton, A. (2022, June 11). *Norse runes: Ultimate guide to the Vikings' Nordic alphabet.* Seek Scandinavia; Houseplant Authority. https://seekscandinavia.com/norse-runes/

Viking runes and runestones. (2014, June 8). History. https://www.historyonthenet.com/viking-runes-and-runestones

Wigington, P. (2008, December 22). *The Norse Runes - A basic overview.* Learn Religions. https://www.learnreligions.com/norse-runes-basic-overview-2562815

Williams, J. A. (n.d.). *The power and mystery of the runes.* Curious Historian https://curioushistorian.com/the-power-and-mystery-of-the-runes

Zhelyazkov, Y. (2022, February 2). *Norse runes explained – meaning and symbolism.* Symbol Sage. https://symbolsage.com/norse-runes-meaning-symbolism/

(N.d.-a). Holisticshop.co.uk. https://www.holisticshop.co.uk/articles/guide-runes

(N.d.-b). Viking-styles.com https://viking-styles.com/blogs/history/runes

20 Children of Odin: Who are they? (2021, May 15). Myth Nerd. https://mythnerd.com/children-of-odin/

Balder – loved by everyone. (n.d.). Historiska.Se. https://historiska.se/norse-mythology/balder-en/

Dan. (2012a, November 14). *Norse mythology for Smart People - the ultimate online guide to Norse mythology and religion.* Norse Mythology for Smart People. https://norse-mythology.org/

Dan. (2012b, November 15). *Bifrost.* Norse Mythology for Smart People. https://norse-mythology.org/cosmology/bifrost/

Dan. (2012c, November 15). *Fenrir.* Norse Mythology for Smart People. https://norse-mythology.org/gods-and-creatures/giants/fenrir/

Dan. (2012d, November 15). *Freyr.* Norse Mythology for Smart People. https://norse-mythology.org/gods-and-creatures/the-vanir-gods-and-goddesses/freyr/

Dan. (2012e, November 15). *Jormungand.* Norse Mythology for Smart People. https://norse-mythology.org/gods-and-creatures/giants/jormungand/

Dan. (2012f, November 15). *Muspelheim.* Norse Mythology for Smart People. https://norse-mythology.org/cosmology/the-nine-worlds/muspelheim/

Dan. (2012g, November 15). *Odin's Discovery of the runes.* Norse Mythology for Smart People. https://norse-mythology.org/tales/odins-discovery-of-the-runes/

Dan. (2012h, November 15). *Ragnarok.* Norse Mythology for Smart People. https://norse-mythology.org/tales/ragnarok/

Dan. (2012i, November 15). *The Creation of Thor's Hammer.* Norse Mythology for Smart People. https://norse-mythology.org/tales/loki-and-the-dwarves/

Dan. (2012j, November 15). *The Death of Baldur.* Norse Mythology for Smart People. https://norse-mythology.org/tales/the-death-of-baldur/

Dan. (2012k, November 15). *The Norns.* Norse Mythology for Smart People. https://norse-mythology.org/gods-and-creatures/others/the-norns/

Dan. (2012l, November 15). *Valhalla.* Norse Mythology for Smart People. https://norse-mythology.org/cosmology/valhalla/

Dan. (2012m, November 15). *Why Odin is one-Eyed.* Norse Mythology for Smart People. https://norse-mythology.org/tales/why-odin-is-one-eyed/

Dan. (2012n, November 15). *Yggdrasil.* Norse Mythology for Smart People. https://norse-mythology.org/cosmology/yggdrasil-and-the-well-of-urd/

Dan. (2014, May 20). *Skoll and Hati.* Norse Mythology for Smart People. https://norse-mythology.org/skoll-hati/

Elly, M. (2018a, May 11). *The punishment of Loki.* BaviPower. https://bavipower.com/blogs/bavipower-viking-blog/the-punishment-of-loki

Elly, M. (2018b, July 6). *Odin's Sons in Norse Myth.* BaviPower. https://bavipower.com/blogs/bavipower-viking-blog/odins-sons-in-norse-myth

Manea, I.-M. (2022). Magic rings in Norse mythology. *World History Encyclopedia.* https://www.worldhistory.org/article/1950/magic-rings-in-norse-mythology/

Mark, J. J. (2021). Sif. *World History Encyclopedia.* https://www.worldhistory.org/Sif/

No title. (n.d.). Study.com. https://study.com/academy/lesson/what-is-norse-mythology-overview-deities-stories.html

www.ingramcontent.com/pod-product-compliance
Lightning Source LLC
Chambersburg PA
CBHW060622310726
48982CB00003B/642

* 9 7 8 1 6 3 8 1 8 1 9 7 2 *